MW01256181

HOW TO *Best* A *Marquess*

RAVEN CLUB SERIES

HOW TO *Best*
A *Marquess*

RAVEN CLUB SERIES

TINA GABRIELLE

This book is a work of fiction. Names, characters, places, and incidents
are the product of the author's imagination or are used fictitiously.
Any resemblance to actual events, locales, or persons, living or dead, is
coincidental.

Copyright © 2019 by Tina Sickler. All rights reserved, including
the right to reproduce, distribute, or transmit in any form or by any
means. For information regarding subsidiary rights, please contact the
Publisher.

Entangled Publishing, LLC
2614 South Timberline Road
Suite 105, PMB 159
Fort Collins, CO 80525
rights@entangledpublishing.com

Scandalous is an imprint of Entangled Publishing, LLC.

Edited by Alycia Tornetta
Cover design by EDH Graphics
Cover photography from Period Images

Manufactured in the United States of America

First Edition July 2019

SCANDALOUS

For Laura and Gabrielle.
My two angels.

Chapter One

April 1825
The Raven Club
An Undisclosed Location in London

Grunts echoed off the paneled walls.

The sickening sounds of flesh hitting flesh.

Ellie Swift's breath stalled in her throat. From the look of things, the boxing match would soon be over. In the center of the large room was a square ring roped off with stakes anchored to the hardwood floor at each corner. In the ring, the two opponents circled each other, rocking back and forth with nimble footwork. Both men were bare-chested and bare-fisted. One fighter was huge, a towering hulk of a man—a well-known pugilist aptly called Bear. The other's back was to her, smooth muscle and bronzed skin glistening beneath the blazing candlelight of the chandeliers. He was tall, just over six feet, but standing in the same ring with Bear seemed to diminish his size.

The crowd cheered, and one could feel the vibrant energy

among the gathered spectators as wagers were swiftly made and money exchanged hands. As far as Ellie could discern, most of the wagers were in favor of Bear.

"Who is he?" Ellie strained to see the mysterious fighter's face from her vantage in the crowd. Her fingers itched to remove her feathered mask to get a better look. But her mask shielded her identity. All the women who attended the Raven Club wore them, especially the wives of wealthy aristocrats who frequented the casino or had a preference for the boxing matches in the back room adjoining the gaming floor. She was drawn to the fights even though her brother, the owner of the club, did not always approve.

She watched, enthralled, as sweat glistened on their brows and backs and ran into the band of their trousers. She'd observed matches before and had seen men's naked chests. She'd roamed the gambling floor and seen her fair share of the pugilists in the boxing room. At twenty-three, she was five years past her first Season, and she'd heard many whispers that she was on her way to becoming a spinster. The whispers hadn't bothered her. She'd much rather spend time in her brother's club than at a ball. Still, despite attending more matches than any young lady should have, she found herself studying the unknown fighter.

"He's a blue blood," a man with a gold front tooth, standing to her right, said.

Nobility? Ellie shifted, but she still couldn't make out his face through the throng of people. Something was familiar about the way he moved—powerful, purposeful...elegant, but she couldn't place him. He had dark hair and broad shoulders. Not uncommon.

"A marquess who likes adventure. Bad that he chose Bear to challenge," a bearded man to her left said.

Bad indeed.

Yet, as she watched, the man's footwork was as swift as

his fists. He ducked and wove and avoided blows that would surely have felled any man if Bear's fists had made contact.

The nagging in the back of her mind continued. What was it about him?

Determined to find out, Ellie wove through the crowd to get closer to the ring. Just as she reached the front, a gasp and shout arose among the crowd. Bear's uppercut connected with his opponent's chin. The dark-haired man's head whipped back, and he staggered, then stumbled forward to catch himself on the ropes.

For a heart-stopping moment, he was inches from her face.

Recognition jolted through her.

Along with a deep-seated dread and a maddening pounding of her heart. The vibrant green of his eyes, the divot in his chin, the full lips, and—

"A kiss from a lovely lady for luck," he said, breathing heavily.

Before she could blink, those perfect lips pressed against hers. Hot. Swift. Over in seconds, he turned to face his opponent.

Ellie, on the other hand, was not as quick to recover.

Oh my God.

It was the devil returned.

Her only consolation was that he didn't recognize her with her mask.

She turned and fled into the refuge of the casino.

• • •

There was something about her.

Hugh Vere, the Marquess of Deveril, did not consider himself a superstitious man. But the lady's kiss had surely turned luck in his favor.

He'd defeated the monster of a man named Bear soon after he'd kissed the lady. Landing a blow to Bear's right temple, his opponent had dropped like a stone.

Hugh wiped his brow with a towel and dipped a dented metal cup in a bucket of water. The cool drink eased his parched throat. He hadn't been in the best position to study the woman closely. His teeth had rattled in his skull after Bear's fist had made jarring contact with his jaw. She'd worn a peacock-feathered mask, and he hadn't made out the color of her eyes. But he had glimpsed her hair. Had it been as vivid a red as he'd thought?

Could it be her?

He'd only known one female who'd had that hair color. The young girl from his past would be a woman now. His brow creased as he tried to recall the details of the masked female he'd kissed moments ago.

He remembered her lips. Soft and inviting. His daring kiss had paid off in a win. Had she stayed to watch?

He tossed the towel to a boy, one of many he'd noticed working at the Raven Club. "The lady with the peacock mask. Who is she?"

The lad shrugged slender shoulders. "No one asks at the Raven, me lord. The ladies wear masks to gamble and watch the fights."

Hugh knew secrecy was prized at the club. It was one of the numerous reasons the place took in a fortune in coin every evening.

"Where did she go?"

The boy pointed to a set of doors at the far end of the cavernous room. "Back to the casino floor."

Hugh had business to conduct at the casino. If he was lucky, he'd spot her on the way and offer his thanks.

The doors led from the boxing room to the main casino floor. It was an ingenious design, in Hugh's opinion. Every vice resided beneath one roof. Almost every vice. From what he'd been told, the Raven Club did not offer demimondes. Only bored widows looking to gamble and some seeking to engage in a night of physical pleasure.

Not much difference in Hugh's estimation. He'd enjoyed the attentions of willing widows and actresses since his return from war months ago.

The casino was busy tonight. Every table on the floor was filled with gamblers hoping to win at a game of chance. The crack of the dice across the green baize of the hazard table drew his eye. The sound of the roulette wheel as the little white ball spun and spun combined with the excited shouts of the players and the call of the croupiers. Men and women gazed at their cards in avaricious intensity at the whist, faro, and *vingt-et-un* tables. Liveried servers with an embroidered *R* on their waistcoats delivered tumblers of amber-colored alcohol on trays to the gamblers. The scent of cigar smoke wafted to him.

He recognized many of the spectators from the boxing match, now eager to spend their winnings on games of chance. Most would lose. Another efficiency of the club he admired. Have them wager on the fights, then pass through the doors and turn around and give their money back to the club at the tables.

"Lord Castleton is waiting for you upstairs," a tall, broad-shouldered man with a brick-like chin said. Hugh had learned his name was Brooks and he was the head guard on the casino floor.

Hugh scanned the room for the red-haired woman in the peacock mask, but she was nowhere to be found. He followed Brooks up a winding staircase to a second floor. The man opened the first door on the right.

It was a spacious room with an oak desk, matching leather chairs, and a thick Oriental carpet. Papers beneath polished stone paperweights and leather-bound ledgers were piled upon the desk. A globe rested on an end table in the corner.

Hugh turned at the sound of a throat clearing to find the earl and his countess standing at the sideboard in the corner of the room.

"Welcome, Lord Deveril. It is a pleasure to see you again." Lady Castleton came forward and curtsied. She was an attractive woman with dark hair and blue eyes. She was also large with child. Her husband, Ian Swift, the Earl of Castleton and the owner of the Raven Club, stood beside his wife.

Hugh hadn't expected the countess to be present. He'd just stepped out of the ring, so he hadn't bothered with a waistcoat and cravat. He wasn't properly attired to meet her.

Hugh bowed. "Thank you, my lady."

"Congratulations on defeating Bear," Lord Castleton said.

Hugh didn't try to hide his surprise. "News travels that quickly?"

"I know everything that happens in the Raven soon after it occurs." Lord Castleton waved toward a window overlooking the casino floor. "I may not be able to see the boxing room, but my workers below deliver messages with simple hand motions. See for yourself."

Hugh walked to a window in the paneled wall that overlooked the casino floor. He could see everything clearly from this vantage point—the flurry of the dealer's hands, the slight sheen of sweat on the gamblers' faces as they placed their wagers, the painted lips of the masked women as they coyly smiled and flirted, and even the satisfied expression of a waiter who received a gold coin after delivering a whisky to a lucky winner.

He was fascinated. It was like a play, the most absorbing performance of human behavior and emotion he'd ever witnessed. It was intoxicating to gaze down and simply watch. No wonder Castleton was considered one of the most powerful men in all of London *before* he'd inherited the earldom.

Hugh coveted the man's good fortune. As well as his dark reputation. Hugh had forsaken his own reputation years ago. After learning of his father and brother's deaths from pneumonia, he'd resigned his army commission and returned to town. He may have taken his place as the Marquess of Deveril, but he no longer cared what others thought, including his miserable mother who currently resided in the country and whom he'd long ago dismissed from his life. When he'd heard rumors that the Raven Club was for sale, he'd reached out to Castleton straightaway.

The door opened, and Hugh turned away from the window.

He froze as the lady with the peacock mask entered. He was able to study her in detail now. Her eyes were a piercing blue from behind the mask. His initial guess had been correct.

Ellie Swift was *here*. And her ringside kiss had given him the luck he'd needed to defeat Bear.

"Ellie," he said aloud before he could stop himself. He experienced a tumult of emotions—joy to see her again, an ache of desire that had never dulled, even through the years, and a heaviness in his chest for all that was lost between them.

Her reaction wasn't as pleasant. She stiffened and shot him a hostile glare. "Good God! What is he doing here?"

"Ellie," Lady Castleton said, in an admonishing tone. "Is that a proper way to greet the marquess?"

Hugh was quick to intervene, and he stepped forward and bowed. "Please, do not make amends. It's lovely to see you again, my lady."

He hadn't been a marquess when they'd first met five years ago. He'd been a second son, untitled and without a shilling to his name. The irony was not lost on him that he'd had to give her up because of his lack of fortune, only to unexpectedly inherit the title and the wealth that accompanied it years later.

Ellie glared at him, then reached up to remove her mask. It was like a punch to the gut. She had changed, grown even more beautiful. Porcelain complexion, red hair the color of a bright sunset, and blue eyes that could devastate a man. The sprinkling of freckles on the bridge of her nose remained. She'd hated them; he'd thought they only added to her perfection.

The last time he'd seen her they had both been eighteen. He'd broken her heart, and she'd fled the gardens of Lady Something-or-other's home with tears in her eyes.

It was a moment he'd relived for years.

"We've asked Lord Deveril here to discuss the future of the Raven Club," Lady Castleton said.

"The future of the club?" From the confused look on Ellie's face, it was clear she had no idea. Why should she? She'd seen him in a boxing ring minutes before and now he was in her brother's private office.

"Lord Deveril seeks to buy the Raven," Castleton said without preamble.

A gasp escaped Ellie, and she pressed a hand to her chest. "You cannot be serious!"

"Ellie," Lord Castleton said, his tone harsh.

She appeared panicked now, and Hugh could not grasp why she had such a strong physical reaction to the news. He knew she hated him, and for good reason, but the Raven Club was business, surely nothing that she should be concerned with.

Ellie's gaze homed in on her brother. "You know I want a chance to take over the Raven. You *promised*."

The Earl of Castleton raised a hand. "I made no such

promise."

Lady Castleton touched her husband's hand. "We said we'd consider it. We know you are more than capable, and with Brooks's continued help to oversee the casino floor, we know the Raven Club would succeed."

Hugh's brow furrowed, and he looked from Ellie to Castleton, then back to Ellie. He was shocked by this turn of events. The earl and countess couldn't possibly consider allowing a young woman to manage London's most notorious gambling club. "You cannot be serious," he said, repeating her phrase. "Ellie is a…is a…"

"A what?" Ellie snapped.

"A lady." The thought of her running the place was ludicrous. How long before someone recognized her behind the frivolous mask? It would be the scandal of the year. Her future would be *ruined*.

"Our first child is expected in a little over a month's time. Once, we never thought to sell the Raven Club, but the years have changed our opinion. I wish to spend time with my wife and child, not a casino," Castleton said.

"I understand," Hugh said.

He didn't. Not really. His parents had been distant to their children and cold toward each other. They had never shared a bedchamber. As far as Hugh knew, the old marquess had visited his wife twice, to have two sons, and never again.

"Whoever takes over must continue the charitable works from the profits," Castleton said.

Hugh knew about the anonymous donations. At first, the earl didn't seem charitable, but as Hugh became better acquainted with the man, he'd realized there was much more to Ian Swift than met the eye. The earl had secrets—deep-seated ones—but what was clear was the fact that he adored his wife.

Hugh had assured the earl and the countess that he

had no qualms about continuing to set aside a portion of the profits for the orphanages and asylums for women as had been established. His reasons for wanting to purchase the Raven Club were twofold: he had a strong interest in boxing, and he had a sharp business mind and knew he could successfully manage the establishment. He valued control, to be in charge. His years as an officer in the military had been regimented, and he'd discovered he was a natural leader.

It hadn't always been this way for him. As a young man, his disciplinarian father had rigidly dictated his future. As a result, Hugh had left for the army, swearing never to allow another to control him. Since inheriting the title and returning from war, he had little patience for high society and had taken on a devil-may-care attitude when it came to the ridiculous rules of the *beau monde*. He wanted more out of life than to simply be a marquess and was determined to choose his own path.

"As I've assured you, I have no protest to donating to the charities. I still want to purchase the establishment."

"No!" Ellie said.

To Hugh's surprise, it was the countess who spoke. "We have considered both of you and have decided to see who would prove the 'best man' for the club. For one month, you will both run the Raven Club. Whoever is most successful will have the establishment. If Ellie wins, she will have the freedom to manage it with Brooks's aid. If Lord Deveril wins, then our solicitors will draw up purchase papers. Your endeavors will be recorded in separate ledgers."

"You think to hold a competition?" Ellie asked in surprise. "That's ludicrous!"

For the first time, Hugh was in agreement with Ellie Swift. He found it hard to believe the earl and countess would even consider such an idea. One look at Castleton's tense expression and Hugh knew it was the countess who had convinced the man to agree to a competition.

Fine. Hugh's gut tightened with a conviction. He'd always been soft where Ellie was concerned. But not in this. It was for her own good.

He *would* win.

"I accept," Hugh said.

. . .

As soon as Hugh left, Ellie faced Ian with fists clenched at her sides.

"How could you do this?" she demanded as indignation swamped her. "You are my *brother*."

"I wanted to say no. I still do. Grace convinced me otherwise," Ian said.

Again, Grace placed a hand on her husband's sleeve. The effect was remarkable. Ian calmed and smiled down at his pregnant wife.

A knot twisted inside Ellie. Once, she thought she'd found a man who had adored her as much as her brother loved her sister-in-law.

That man had been Hugh Vere, now known as the Marquess of Deveril. She'd dubbed him the devil marquess, for certainly that was an apt name.

What a fool she'd been. Only eighteen, she'd just had her debut into Society and attended her first ball. She'd met an equally young and handsome Hugh, second son to the Marquess of Deveril. He hadn't minded her red hair, freckles, or her love of books. They'd been drawn to each other and had quickly fallen in love.

Or rather, *she'd* fallen madly in love with *him*.

"You know about our past," Ellie said.

Her brother and sister-in-law knew most, not all. She could never confess every humiliating moment. She'd cried in private for over a year. Her younger sister, Olivia, had attempted to comfort her during many dark and lonely nights, but Ellie had wept until she'd been exhausted and fallen into a restless sleep. Even Ian and Grace had tried to cheer her on more than one trip to Gunter's for ices but had been unable to pull Ellie out of her melancholy.

It had taken years to harden her heart.

"You are no longer eighteen. You've rejected suitor after suitor ever since," Ian said.

"I will only marry for love. Just like you with Grace."

It was an excuse. She didn't want to marry. She wanted to run the Raven Club and become an independent woman. Only then could she continue to use her good fortune to help others—women who were at the mercy of men who were sworn to protect and cherish them, not hurt them. If she ever chose a husband, then she preferred one who could be easily managed and fooled, who would never be a risk to her heart.

"I support your decision to choose your own husband, but not in this." Her brother waved his hand to the window overlooking the casino floor. "This is no life for a young lady."

Grace cleared her throat. "Contrary to my husband's opinion, I do believe a woman has what it takes to run the Raven Club."

"I knew you would take my side," Ellie said, hope lifting her spirits.

Grace was talented with figures and took over the bookkeeping soon after she'd wed Ian. She'd also been teaching Ellie, who much preferred numbers and books over balls and dandies.

And rogues like Hugh.

She'd heard rumors of him in the ladies' retiring room since his return from the army and his ascension to the title. He rarely attended the same events she did, so she hadn't seen him. But his reputation for scandal preceded him. Widows.

Actresses. Dancers. The salacious rumors had confirmed everything he'd done to her.

Grace shook her head. "I haven't taken anyone's side yet. But Ian and I have reached a compromise. A test, if you prefer. Whoever is most successful in one month's time shall have the Raven."

"You would choose Deveril over your own flesh and blood?"

Ian let out a puff of air. "Cease the dramatics, Ellie. This is business. If not for my wife's urging, I would have had my solicitor draw up the papers a week ago. Now do you accept or not?"

"Fine," Ellie snapped. "I accept."

Chapter Two

Ellie found Hugh leaning against a wall outside of Ian's office. He straightened when she stepped outside, all six feet four inches of him. His dark brown hair was mussed from his recent fight in the ring. An image returned in a rush—broad shoulders and bronze skin glistening from physical exertion, muscles bunching and straining as he punched and jabbed at his opponent.

Barbaric. Predatory.

Arousing.

By sheer force of will, she pushed the image aside.

"Why? Why would you possibly want the Raven Club?" she asked without preamble.

"Why wouldn't I? It's a solid investment, I have talent in the ring, and I have a head for business."

"Rumor says you have a head for scandal."

"Ah, you've been following me?" His lips curled in a lazy grin, and his green eyes darkened a shade, reminding her of the ferns that flourished in the summer on her family's country estate.

Five years ago, those eyes would have charmed. His lips would have seduced. Her fingers would have tingled with the need to touch and trace the enticing divot in his chin. His features no longer held a youthful attractiveness but had grown into a man's—a very handsome one's.

But she was no longer attracted to scoundrels, and he was the worst kind. She hadn't followed him, as he'd suggested, but neither had she ignored the whispers in the ladies' retiring rooms.

"Do not flatter yourself, my lord. I haven't been following you, only aware that you left your military career to ascend to the title." She lowered her voice an octave. "I was sorry to hear about your father and brother."

His expression stilled and grew serious, and despite everything that had occurred between them, she felt a pang of sympathy for his loss. "Thank you."

"But I must admit, I often wondered if I'd hear news of your demise on the battlefield." For years, she'd secretly dreaded news of his death. She'd never heard from him, not one single letter. And now he was back in her life, determined to wreak havoc once again.

His smile did not reach his eyes. "Ah, I'm sorry to disappoint you."

She folded her arms across her chest and tapped her foot, her mood veering sharply back to anger. "Your history does not explain your presence here today. Of all the gaming clubs in London, why this one?"

"The Raven Club is well known."

"So? You must have known my brother owns it."

He stalked closer, his movements smooth. She struggled not to step back. "Your brother, yes. I had no idea *you* came with the place."

She tossed her hair behind her shoulder. His gaze followed the movement. "I happen to want the Raven."

He had the audacity to laugh. The sound was rich and echoed off the paneled walls, releasing a slew of memories she'd locked up in a hidden chamber in her heart.

Hugh laughing and teasing her. Hugh tickling her. Hugh smiling right before he kissed her and told her he loved her.

Liar. Scoundrel. *Blackguard.*

She straightened her spine. There was too much at stake to lose to him. The club aided the charities. Hugh said he didn't mind and would continue the efforts. But there was more, much more behind her motivations. She had made strides in helping the women who came to the club and sought her aid, beaten women who had nowhere else to go. If Hugh acquired the place, all her efforts would be for naught.

"I want to ask the same of you. Why do you want the place?" he asked.

She had to tread carefully, had to think of a reason a man like Hugh would believe. She'd never tell him the true reasons. She suspected he wouldn't approve of her plans, and telling him was a risk she wasn't willing to take. "It belongs to my family."

One dark eyebrow shot up. "And?"

"And I have a good head for business," she said, throwing his words back at him.

"It doesn't make sense."

"Why? Because I'm a woman? You think ladies aren't intelligent or capable of running a business?"

"No. I don't doubt your intelligence. I never have. I remember your fondness for books."

More memories assailed her. Memories of Hugh stealing a kiss in her family's library. He'd claimed he was as attracted to her intelligence as much as he was to her red hair and freckles. He'd lied about that as well. She'd heard the whispers of other women; her shade of hair and her freckles were too bold to be pretty, and men preferred subtle and perfected beauty.

Hugh's behavior had reaffirmed those whispers. The lady she'd caught him kissing in the gardens, Miss Isabelle West, had been a green-eyed, voluptuous brunette. Not one freckle had marred her pert nose.

"If you don't doubt my intelligence, then you should understand my ambitions," she said.

"No, I do not. Nothing changes the fact that you are a lady. An earl's sister. You risk others discerning your identity. What of your reputation?"

Her hackles rose. "What of yours? A marquess who owns a gambling club?"

His brows snapped together in disapproval. "It's not the same. Your idea is ludicrous."

Hugh's high-handed manner inflamed her further. "Ludicrous or not, we are in competition. One month to show who can run this place. I plan on winning." She *had* to win.

He leaned close, too close, and his lips curled in a smile. "Challenge accepted."

· · ·

"Where to, miss?" the hackney driver asked.

Ellie gave an address, then lowered the shade a few inches. The hackney started with a jerk, and Ellie leaned back on the seat. An hour after leaving Hugh, she'd departed from the back of the Raven Club and walked to the end of the street to hail a hackney. Evading a chaperone had not been difficult. Her family assumed she was ensconced in the office looking over the club's ledgers.

Fifteen minutes later, she arrived at her destination. The Cock and Bull Tavern.

Ellie stepped outside the hackney and paid the driver. Picking up her skirts, she crossed the street and waited outside. The tavern was a two-story red brick structure with a large bay window. An old man smoking a clay pipe stood outside the door, and a few drunken revelers walked the street.

A carriage pulled up, its harnesses rattling. Black and nondescript, no one paid it much heed on the street. The window shade parted a few inches, and a woman peered out.

Time to go.

Ellie hurried across the street. Not waiting for the driver to jump down and offer aid, she opened the door of the black carriage and stepped inside.

Violet Lasher sat on the padded bench, her voluminous skirts splayed about her. No matter how many times Ellie was in her presence, she stared. Violet was stunning, with blond hair, a porcelain complexion, and sapphire eyes. Her artfully cut bodice displayed the mounds of her breasts and slender waist. Diamonds glittered at her throat and ears. Ellie didn't doubt they were real, not glass.

Violet Lasher was the highest-paid courtesan in London.

"Were you followed?" Violet asked.

"No."

"Not by the marquess?"

"Definitely not."

Ellie had penned a note telling Violet her predicament over the Raven Club and her challenge to win the establishment from the Marquess of Deveril.

"Good. We must keep these meetings secret." Violet smoothed her skirts, and a ring winked on every finger, diamonds and emeralds. "Rose Belise is safely ensconced in Scotland by now."

"Scotland?"

"A vicar's wife needed a companion. Rose was pleased to go."

"And her husband, the earl?"

"Drunk and raving mad. Looking for his wife's lover, whom he believes is responsible for her disappearance."

"Rose didn't have a lover," Ellie pointed out.

Violet shrugged a slender shoulder. "Not that the earl knows. If he discovers the truth behind his wife's escape, he'll come looking for the person responsible at the Raven Club."

"He won't. Rose claimed his brain isn't as large as other parts of him."

Violet's lips curled in a smile, then her expression sobered. "Still. There is the possibility that you put yourself in danger."

"So do you."

Violet laughed, a throaty feminine sound that no doubt had lured dozens of men to their knees. "I can handle a man."

Ellie envied her power. Violet may be a courtesan, never a wife, but she had an abundance of beauty *and* brains. She'd also never be a slave to a man as his wife, never lose her property or her name upon marriage.

Most importantly, never lose her heart.

When Violet grew old, she was shrewd enough to have saved a tidy fortune and a small home in Brighton by the sea—a home that was a gift from a grateful, aging noble.

Fortunately for Ellie, the courtesan also had a conscience and was her accomplice in aiding the abused and desperate women who came to Ellie at the club. Violet's sister had been beaten to death by her husband. He'd never stood trial for his crime and even remarried. Violet had been ten years younger than her sister and helpless to obtain justice for her murder.

She eventually had her vengeance by paying a man to slice her brother-in-law's throat and drop him in the Thames.

The courtesan tilted her head to the side and regarded Ellie. "Why do you put yourself at risk? Was it a friend?"

Ellie's fingers tightened on the strings of her reticule. She knew what the courtesan was asking. "Mary wasn't a friend.

At least, not right away."

"Then why?"

Ellie hesitated, but Violet had a way of putting her at ease. "Lady Moore, Mary, frequented the club. My brother, Ian, first noticed the bruises. He refused her husband, a viscount, membership. She came to the club more often then, knowing she would be safe for those few hours. Mary was only a year older than myself at the time, and I recalled seeing her when I had my own debut. We all thought her fortunate when the viscount proposed to her so early. She had two sons soon after her marriage. But when she showed up at the club a few years later we became friends and she told me...stories. Disturbing ones." Ellie cleared her throat and swallowed. "The viscount had a horrible temper."

"Her children?"

The words came easier now. "She'd purposely taunt the viscount during his fits to protect her two boys. She'd take beatings for them. Ian offered to smuggle her out of London, to find a new life for her on the continent, but she refused. She couldn't leave her children." Divorce was nearly impossible, especially for the aristocracy. It required an act of Parliament, and the wife would lose all rights to her children. Ellie thought it horribly unfair, a legal system created by men for their benefit at the sacrifice of women.

"I can surmise the ending," Violet said, a note of sadness in her voice.

"My friend was found dead at the bottom of the grand staircase in their London home. Her neck was broken. The viscount claimed a burglar had pushed her from the top step." Ellie's voice broke. "She should have run. The end result would have been the same. Her children remain at their father's mercy."

News of Mary's death had been a turning point for Ellie. She'd decided to help as much as she could.

"You cannot save everyone," Violet said.

"I'm not foolish enough to believe I can. But I can continue my efforts. I'm expanding the club to have a private gambling room for women. I have no doubt it will be profitable. Many wealthy women frequent the club for entertainment. But I have another motive as well, one that involves subterfuge. I've arranged for a hidden room to be connected to the women's gambling room, a bedchamber where a woman can spend the night until she can be moved."

"And the Marquess of Deveril? How do you expect to accomplish all this without his knowledge? I can only assume he will want to know what his competition is accomplishing."

"He will never learn of the hidden room." She'd keep it from Hugh at all costs.

Violet leaned back on the padded bench. "Hmm. Not all gentlemen are bad. There are those that cherish their wives and their marital bonds."

Ellie knew that. Ian cherished Grace. He couldn't wait for their babe to be born.

"The Devil Marquess is not one of those men," Ellie snapped.

Violet arched a well-plucked eyebrow. "You think he'd hurt a woman?"

"No, not physically." Of that, she was certain. He might be a blackguard, but deep in the marrow of her bones, she knew he'd never strike a woman. "But there are other types of harm."

"Ah, he broke your heart years ago."

Damn Violet for being so uncannily perceptive. "I am no longer a lovesick girl who swoons over a pair of green eyes."

"I have no doubt you can challenge him for the casino. But beware, a heart is a tricky organ. It has a will of its own," Violet said.

"You needn't fear. This heart is immune to the Devil Marquess."

Chapter Three

"Early start, Ellie?"

Ellie turned to see Hugh leaning against a macao table, arms folded across his chest. Unlike yesterday, he was dressed in a green coat and striped waistcoat. The color highlighted the chips of green in his eyes, and the meticulous tailoring of his clothing emphasized his broad shoulders. After the boxing match, she knew firsthand his coat was not padded.

She was surprised to find him here. It was still morning, and the club was closed. Only a few staff were present to clean and prepare for the evening. The fresh scent of lemon polish was redolent in the air. Even Ian and his man, Brooks, were not in sight.

"Why are you here so early?" she asked. "I assumed you would have spent a late evening easing your bruises from the boxing match with a lady of the night."

An infuriating smirk appeared on his handsome face. "I'm sorry to disappoint you, Ellie, but I spent a pleasant evening in my home. Alone."

"Shocking."

"Not so. I was pondering how best to increase the club's profitability."

Damn. He was taking this seriously. Curiosity rose within her. Just what were his plans? She knew better than to ask outright. She'd have to watch him from a distance and try to discern his tactics. Meanwhile, she had her own work to accomplish. She planned to keep track of every shilling of her profits in her ledgers. She assumed he would do the same with his own. It would not be difficult to determine which of them had out-earned the other by the end of the time period.

"I shall leave you to your ill-fated plans then." She made to step by him, but he unfolded his arms, pushed away from the table, and placed a hand on her sleeve.

At the simple touch, her pulse fluttered alarmingly. Even through her clothing, her skin tingled from the warmth.

"After your adamant speech yesterday, I would think you'd start straightaway. Where are you headed?" Hugh asked.

"My affairs are none of your concern."

"Not true. We are in competition, remember?"

"How could I forget?" She resisted the urge to remove his hold with her free hand. Even gloved, she didn't want to touch him.

"I must keep an eye on you and your efforts. You can do the same and keep me close, of course."

She narrowed her eyes and glared at him. She understood the need to unearth his battle plans regarding the club, but spending time with Hugh was the last thing she desired. *Why would he want to keep me close?* a warning voice whispered in her head. Did he have a hidden purpose? Was he using the competition to try to seduce her like one of his conquests?

Heat bloomed inside her at the thought. Her muscles tensed, and her breathing grew rapid. A tingling warmth spread through her body. She hated her reaction to him.

She pushed the thought of his seduction aside. Taking a step back, she pulled her arm from his grasp. It made no sense. *He* had been the one to end their romance years ago. "I must protest your efforts. Watching each other would defeat the purpose of competition, wouldn't it?"

"Nonsense. We only have one month. Anyone would want to discern their opponent's objectives. Envision an invisible rope around your waist and tied to mine. That's how close I intend to keep you."

An invisible rope? Once more, the idea of Hugh pursuing her rose in her mind.

No. She knew his game. He was trying to intimidate her, get her to withdraw from the competition.

Devil. She didn't fear him, not one bit. She had much more mettle than when they'd first met.

She raised her chin and met his gaze. "Fine. But do not feel bad when I best you."

"Oh, I don't intend to lose. I never do."

Something in his tone sent a ripple down her spine. Was he talking about the club, or heaven help them, *her*?"

He stepped closer, closing the distance she'd purposely put between them. "You can follow me today, or I shall follow you. Your choice, Ellie."

That's not much of a choice!

She made a quick assessment. He'd learn of the private women's gaming room soon enough. Workers would have to paint the room, decorations and furnishings would have to be purchased and delivered. Gambling tables ordered and installed. She saw no harm in showing him now. At least, she could reveal the main room.

The second chamber would remain hidden.

She left him to walk to one of the roulette tables. Her hand grazed the walnut finish.

He followed. "You plan to add another roulette table or

replace this one with another game of chance?" Hugh asked.

"No. You see only this room, but there is more." Ellie turned to press a latch in a paneled wall across from the roulette table. She felt a *click*, then a section of the panel opened to reveal a door leading into a chamber. He followed her inside.

"A hidden room," he said, looking impressed.

She swept inside, and he was right behind her.

"The club has many. There are also private rooms for gamblers who desire private high-stakes games. This one was unused," she said. It was a significant space, wide enough to fit several gaming tables, settees, chairs, and end tables. Only one roulette table currently sat in the center of the room.

He walked the perimeter of the room, seeming to scan the space and measure it in his mind. "Will you use it for higher-stakes games?"

"In a sense. But only for women. Ladies will be free to remove their masks if they choose or to keep them on. The servants at the Raven Club are sworn to secrecy."

"Ah, you feel the women need their own room."

"They will be free to join the gentlemen on the main casino floor or to enter here. I believe once it becomes known, many more ladies will seek membership."

"Fascinating. I see I have much more competition than I'd initially believed."

"You didn't take me seriously?"

He grinned. "Perhaps."

She leaned against the roulette table and feigned interest in the green baize. His answer irked her. For some reason, it was important to her that he take her seriously. She knew that didn't make sense. Not when she could use his prejudice to her advantage. If he thought her an unworthy opponent, then she could fool him into believing she was incompetent and swoop in to win the Raven after her well-laid plans filled the club's coffers with coin.

"Will female servants serve the women here?" he asked.

It was a harmless question, but she seized the opportunity to provoke him. Maybe he'd leave her alone and she could see to her work with the hidden back room.

She looked away from the roulette table to meet his eyes. "Of course not. I will personally select the most virile of our servants to work here."

His grin faltered. "The most virile?"

Oh, how wonderful it was to wipe the smug smile from his face. "Yes."

His posture stiffened, enough for her to notice. "You intend to select them?"

She blinked innocently. "Must you repeat everything I say?"

"What will your brother think?"

"He will not know all my efforts, only the outcome."

One dark eyebrow shot up. "Remember what I said about an invisible rope tying us together?"

Somehow, he'd turned things around, and she felt an uncomfortable tightening in her chest. She would have stepped back were she not leaning on the gaming table beside her. "You know of my plans now. No sense following me as I carry them out."

His grin surprised her. Straight white teeth flashed in his handsome face. Her cheeks grew warm, and a tingling began at the base of her neck. The large room suddenly felt very small. What was it about him that unnerved her so easily?

"I can think of nothing better than following you about. Someone has to watch you."

If she had a fireplace poker, she'd hit him. It probably wouldn't make a dent in his dense skull.

"I am no longer a child."

His gaze roved her lazily from her lips to her bodice down

to her feet, then back up to her eyes. "Oh, I'm very aware of that fact."

Her already warm cheeks grew alarmingly hot, along with other parts of her that she refused to acknowledge. Her eyes became riveted on his angular jaw and wide, sensual mouth. "And you? What are your plans?"

He rested a hand on the table beside her. His fingers were long and tapered, his knuckles calloused, certainly not the hands of a marquess. He didn't cage her in, but neither did he stand a respectable distance from her. She could feel the heat of his body and smell the crisp, masculine scent of his cologne.

"Prizefighting. The club makes a tiny sum from the fights. The winners then gamble their winnings on the tables, promptly returning it to the club."

She knew this. She also knew prizefighting was against the law, but that didn't stop men and even women from attending the fights in droves.

"To start, I intend to increase the number of fights and invite champions like Gentleman Jackson, Tom Crib, Jem Belcher, Bill Richmond, and even American Tom Molyneux," he said.

"You think they'd box here?"

"No. But they'd attend. People would line up to show off their skills knowing one of the champions was in attendance. Thousands of spectators attend Fives Court in Leicester Fields in St. Martin's Lane to watch the sparring matches. I don't expect to rival that number, but plenty will come if they know the champions will referee or simply watch."

This was an unexpected tactic that even her brother hadn't thought of, and a part of her was concerned. Would Hugh's efforts exceed hers? Would they be more profitable?

She pushed the thought aside. Her plans must come to fruition. The women needed her. She couldn't afford to lose. "I also insist on learning everything else you plan. An invisible rope, remember?" She tossed the words back at him, but instead of having the intended result, Hugh's lips curled into a knowing smile.

"I'm counting on it."

• • •

She was going to drive him mad.

The most virile servers.

The idea of young men lining up for Ellie's perusal... It was reckless and scandalous. Where was her chaperone?

More importantly, where was her brother, Castleton? Hugh knew without a doubt the earl had no notion of his sister's plans. Most likely, he believed she'd ensconce herself in the office surrounded by thick ledgers while she gave orders to the burly guard, Brooks, on how best to run the establishment. The earl probably believed his sister would rarely step foot on the casino floor.

They'd all been wrong. Her idea of a women's gambling room was impressive. God knew, he'd encountered his fair share of ladies, widows and married ones, who sought out adventure. In his case, they'd blatantly propositioned him for a night of pleasure. He'd obliged the widows. As for married ladies, he'd never stick his prick up their skirts. Not when there were plenty of others, women who knew his expectations and would not place demands on him.

But Ellie was different.

Special.

For as long as he lived, he'd never forget the girl of his youth.

He wanted the Raven Club for his own purposes. The boxing was a strong draw for him, just as enticing as the business. He found stepping into the ring and facing an opponent exhilarating and fair after experiencing five years in the military where battles were often unfairly fought and soldiers often faced opponents ill-equipped, outnumbered, and unprepared. He was in control in the ring, and he craved the same control over his future. Owning the club was the key to ensuring power over his fate. His title wasn't enough. It had belonged to his brother, and he'd never coveted it.

Yes, he wanted the club, but now he wanted to protect Ellie as well.

Damn.

What was she thinking?

He'd broken her heart in the past, not because he'd wanted to, but because he'd *had* to. His mind slipped into the past. His father's words echoed in his head.

"I forbid you to marry the girl. I will not have the marquessate associated with that family. There are rumors Castleton was responsible for his brother's death to gain the earldom. He still owns that sinful gambling club. Stay away from the Castleton chit. If not, you won't get a shilling from me, boy. Do you understand? Not a shilling. You think she will want to live as a beggar on her own family?"

No amount of pleading had worked. His parents had always been cold and harsh, and the marquess and marchioness had been adamant. Do as he was told or suffer the consequences. He'd had no power then, no choice, and he'd hated it.

Could he be that selfish? Could he marry Ellie with empty pockets? He'd only been eighteen years old, yet he'd known the answer. Hugh had too much pride to beg to his brother-in-law, the Earl of Castleton, for the rest of their lives. Ellie had been raised in luxury. She'd never gone without the finer things in life. Dresses and jewels. Balls, garden parties, theaters, and operas. Champagne toasts and six-course dinners. She may have been willing to give that up, but would she have grown to regret her decision?

Would she have come to resent him?

He'd done what was right for her then. He'd met Miss Isabelle West, who was now Lady Fabry upon her marriage to an old earl, in the gardens that fateful night. He knew what the outcome would be. He hated the kiss, hated every damned second of it. Isabelle had clung to him like a vine, and he'd felt nothing but revulsion. Yet, he hadn't pushed her away and knew Ellie would find them.

In hindsight, he'd sacrificed Ellie in vain. If only he'd known he'd inherit the title. The fact had left a painful knot inside him for years. But he didn't regret looking out for Ellie.

He'd done what was best for her then.

He wouldn't cease now.

• • •

"Oh, Ellie. Did it have to be Hugh Vere?"

Ellie cringed at her younger sister's words. It was after the evening meal, and Ellie sat on the window seat in Olivia's bedchamber.

"I'm not happy with the turn of events," Ellie said.

Olivia knew all about her troubled past with Hugh. Just like Ellie, Olivia had been surprised to learn of Ian and Grace's decision regarding the club.

Olivia joined her on the window seat and took Ellie's hand. At twenty-one, Olivia was two years younger. With her fair hair and green eyes, their coloring was different. Their features, however, were similar, although Olivia didn't have freckles on the bridge of her nose. Where Ellie was concerned with the Raven Club, Olivia had a fondness for horses, riding, and adventure. On more than one occasion, she'd eagerly waited for Ian to return from a trip to Tattersall's to examine the horses he'd purchased. Although Olivia didn't race, she often talked of it, and it made Ellie worry. Horse racing was how their oldest brother had died, thrown from his mount on a treacherous track.

"It's been five years. What is he like now? Has his appearance changed?" Olivia asked.

"Yes and no. He's taller." Ellie swallowed. "And bigger."

"He's fat?"

"No. Just...bigger." Unbidden images of Hugh in the boxing ring returned. There wasn't a pinch of fat on his torso. As for his height, Ellie had reached her full height by seventeen. Hugh, it seemed, was several inches taller since she'd last seen him.

"Why does he want the Raven Club?" Olivia asked.

"He has a preference for boxing. That's where I first saw him. Bare-fisted, prizefighting in the back of the casino."

"No gloves? Truly?"

"Yes." Heat simmered in her veins, and she feared she'd dream of him in the ring tonight. Almost all of the pugilists wore gloves, but Hugh had stepped into the ring with Bear without them. She cleared her throat. "He also claims it is a good business investment."

"He is a marquess now. They don't dabble in trade."

The only reason their brother owned the Raven Club was because he'd been tossed out of their father's home and needed a means to survive. Ian, like Hugh, had been born a second son of an aristocratic family. Neither were supposed to inherit their family titles.

But unlike Ian, Hugh had been an officer when his father and older brother had died, leaving Hugh to ascend to the marquessate. He did not need the Raven Club for income.

So what were his true motives? She didn't trust the Devil Marquess, not one inch.

"You should know that it was Grace who convinced Ian to hold the competition," Olivia said.

Ellie was grateful to her sister-in-law. Grace understood a woman's need to have more in her life than marriage, understood a woman's ambitions of financial independence from a man. Grace had secretly managed the ledgers of a widowed milliner before she'd married their brother. After the wedding, she'd taken over handling the club's ledgers.

"I would ask why Lord Deveril never married, but they say he prefers actresses over eligible young ladies," Olivia said.

Ellie had heard the same. Still, she asked, "Where did you hear this?"

"In the ladies' retiring room at Lady Holloway's ball. It's astonishing what women talk about after relieving themselves."

"Olivia!" Ellie attempted to admonish her younger sister but ended up chuckling instead.

"Rumors say the head actress of Drury Lane was his paramour at one time," Olivia said.

Ellie held up a hand. She didn't want to hear more. The Hugh she recalled was young and earnest and affectionately loyal. He'd never flirted or danced with other ladies. Nor were there any whispers about transgressions or liaisons with seasoned actresses.

Until she'd found him kissing another lady.

Perhaps he'd been better at hiding his true nature then. Or he'd more recently begun to realize the delights of actresses' off-stage skills?

"Meanwhile, do you plan to continue your work with Violet Lasher?" Olivia asked.

Her sister knew about her efforts. Olivia never judged, and Ellie was grateful for her confidence. Olivia's sense of adventure had aided Ellie. "I do. It is too important to set aside while I beat the Devil Marquess at his own game."

"Good. I've met a friend. Lady Willoughby."

"Baron Willoughby's young wife?"

"Yes. Lady Willoughby...Samantha, as I call her...is my age. I had sent her an invitation to join me for afternoon tea. The baron appeared in the vestibule and caused quite a commotion. He insisted on seeing his wife. I believe he thought she was having a secret liaison. Samantha paled at the sight of her towering husband in the parlor doorway. I actually feared she would faint from fear. He fetched her in a most ungentlemanly way by grasping her arm and ushering her to his carriage."

"You think Lord Willoughby hurts his wife?"

"I do."

"Do they have children?"

"Thank heavens, no. Not yet. I suggested she attend the Raven Club with me one evening. She adamantly refused. She probably fears her husband will learn of her visit and punish her."

Her sister's words weighed heavily upon Ellie. Her breath turned shallow, and she swallowed the sudden lump that appeared in her throat. "You have done all you can."

Olivia paled. "I dread it is not enough. If my suspicions are correct and harm befalls her, I fear I will never forgive myself."

If Ellie had any say, that wouldn't happen.

Chapter Four

"Good morning, Brooks. I plan to go shopping, and I'll need Alice," Ellie said as she stepped into the vestibule and spotted Brooks the following morning.

Her brother's longtime friend was an invaluable part of the casino. He roamed the floor each evening and worked many tasks, from guarding the door to overseeing the croupiers to announcing the boxing matches in the boxing room. He was also the largest man Ellie had ever seen and had a chest the size of a small armoire. If she won the club, he would oversee the casino floor while she worked above in the office. With his help, she needn't don her mask and visit the casino floor every night.

"Of course. I'll send for Alice at once." Brooks's broad shoulders disappeared around the corner.

Moments later, Alice appeared. A tall, thin-boned woman in her early fifties, she smiled when she saw Ellie. "Where to today, miss?"

"I require items for the women's gaming room." Ellie needed not only furnishings and curtains for the main room, but also items for the secret hidden room, specifically a bed.

"I'll fetch my cloak." Alice hurried off.

Alice had served as a ladies' maid in a wealthy man's home until her employer had begun pursuing her. When Alice refused his advances, he sent her packing without a reference. After Ian heard her story, he immediately hired her to work at the Raven. It wasn't uncommon. Grace and Ian often used the club for good. Ellie preferred Alice because she was discreet and never raised an eyebrow about Ellie's unconventional activities.

Ellie was in the process of pulling on her gloves when the distinct sound of boot heels on the marble vestibule made her turn as Hugh approached. "Where are you going?"

She frowned. "Must you question my every movement?"

"Invisible rope, remember?"

How can I forget?

She tapped her foot impatiently. "I plan on visiting the drapers. If you wish to accompany me, then by all means, who am I to refuse such masculine companionship?"

His only reaction was a twitch to his left eyebrow. Good. Most men despised shopping, and trailing behind her in the drapers as she selected fabrics, curtains, table linens, and trimmings would bore any red-blooded male.

But her victory was short-lived when a smile tugged at his lips, and he extended his arm. "I can think of no better way to spend a pleasant morning."

"You're jesting."

"Never. As I said, I must keep an eye on your efforts."

Her thoughts churned as she considered this change of plans. His presence would certainly curtail her additional purchases, items she needed to furnish the hidden room. Frustration roiled in her gut. She was aware of him watching her, so she was careful to school her expression.

"Of course," she said, forcing a pleasant tone.

Just then, Alice appeared with her cloak.

"Alice, Lord Deveril will be accompanying us this morning."

The woman curtsied, then turned and crooked an eyebrow in question at her mistress. Ellie shrugged.

When they stepped outside, Ellie waved for a hackney.

"No. We shall make use of my carriage," Hugh said.

"That's not necessary."

"You would turn down a perfectly good carriage? Don't be surly, or do you fear being in close quarters with me?"

Swine. She met his green gaze. "Of course not."

"Good." His carriage was summoned, and moments later, two perfectly matched bays appeared pulling a black carriage. His family crest was emblazoned on the side door. He helped Alice alight, but when it was Ellie's turn, his hand lingered on her arm and then grazed her lower back. A shiver thundered down her spine.

Stop! He has no power over you.

Alice sat in the corner, and Ellie had no choice but to sit across from the marquess. There was a lurch as the carriage started rolling. Planning to ignore him for the journey, she raised the tasseled shade and looked out the window.

"Why did you never marry?"

Her gaze snapped to his. This was not a topic of conversation she desired to engage in with him. It was definitely *not* a question a gentleman would ask a lady. From the corner of her eye, she spotted Alice stiffen but remain silent. Ellie boldly met his intense stare with her own. "Why didn't you?"

"I prefer bachelorhood."

"I prefer my unmarried life as well."

"Liar. All women seek a husband."

Her fingers clenched her skirts. Damn him. He had no right to inquire why she'd never married, not after their past. She raised her chin a notch. "Perhaps you have met the exceptional female."

His eyes traveled over her face, then onto her mouth. He hesitated, then met her gaze, but not before causing her to shift in her seat. Leaning close so that her maid would not hear, he whispered, "Perhaps, but I have to admit that I've always found exceptions fascinating."

A knot rose in her throat. How was she to respond to that? He had a maddening knack for taking her off guard and gaining the upper hand. It didn't help that he was looking at her like she was a rarity that he did indeed find fascinating. Nor did it help her pounding pulse that she was strangely flattered by his interest.

She glanced at Alice, but thankfully, the woman had not heard his last words.

She was saved from answering when he glanced out the window. "We have arrived."

Thank my lucky stars!

She looked out the window to see Grafton House at 164 New Bond Street, a well-known London linen draper. Colorful fabrics and trimmings were artfully displayed in the bay window to entice customers to enter.

Hugh hopped out of the carriage and waved away the driver to lower the step himself. This time, Ellie was careful not to touch him as she descended. If he noticed, he didn't mention it.

The bells above the shop's doors tinkled as they stepped inside. Bolts of fabric in what seemed like every color of the rainbow crammed the shelves—linens, muslins, broadcloth, violets, and crepes. The shop was a kaleidoscope of color and texture. A handful of women perused the wares as workers aided them with their selections.

Alice waited at the front of the shop as Ellie flitted through the rows of shelves displaying household linens of sheets, table linens, curtains, and bath cloths. She removed her gloves and tucked them into her reticule so that she could touch and feel the weight and texture of each fabric. Hugh trailed close, never far behind her.

She recalled his words in the carriage. This wouldn't do. She had to stop thinking of Hugh Vere in a sexual fashion. She couldn't allow him to distract her. She'd worked hard for her chance to prove her worth to her brother and sister-in-law. Financial independence and the chance to run the Raven were much more meaningful than an infuriating marquess.

She brought her mind back to her task at hand. The women's gambling room required many items, and she'd best get started. She reached for a bolt of red velvet perfect for lush curtains. She could envision the decor as a splendid contrast to the green baize of the tables.

"I would avoid that color," Hugh said.

She scowled at him over her shoulder. "Why? It would make for a dramatic effect for curtains in my women's gambling room."

"No. It would resemble a house of ill repute."

She blinked. The only reason he'd know that is if he'd visited one of the bordellos in London himself.

"May I suggest a subtler color." He reached for a bolt of light blue silk. "Now this resembles a lovely sky. Feel the texture."

The silk swept across her bare fingers like a wisp of a cloud—soft and delicate. It tickled her senses and heightened her awareness of both the fabric and the man.

His fingers brushed hers as he took the fabric from her. "The trick is to let the gamblers feel like they are outside, without ever having to leave."

She'd heard Ian say the same thing. *Keep the patrons inside as long as possible. The more time in the club, the more money they will wager.*

Maybe Hugh had what it took to run the Raven Club.

"What do you think?" he asked.

Under his steady scrutiny, she struggled to think. "The casino floor lacks windows for a reason. If the gamblers cannot look outside, then they often forget the time, how long they have been at the tables, and will remain to place bets."

"A common trick among all gambling halls."

Her thoughts came easier now. "Blue silk curtains will let them think time has not passed. I concur with your suggestion."

He pressed a hand to his chest in mock surprise. "I'm astonished."

She scowled. "Do not let it go to your head."

"Never," he swore.

She laughed. She couldn't help herself, then clasped a hand over her mouth.

He stiffened and stared. "I like the sound of your laughter. You used to laugh all the time."

At the mention of their past, she quieted, and her heart went cold and still. Whether he meant it or not, it was a reminder of why she was here, why she must never lose her wits around him or forget her goals. He must have sensed the tension within her, for he set down the silk and turned the topic of conversation.

"Have you decided what games of chance will be in your women's salon?" he asked.

She lowered her hand to touch the silk. "Not yet. And I wouldn't tell you anyway."

"*Tsk*. That's not nice."

"Nice? We are in competition."

He leaned close and lowered his voice. "From my experience, competition brings out passion."

Passion? The world rolled lushly off his lips, and her heart leaped wildly in response. She clenched her fist, crushing a handful of delicate silk. "You should not speak to me that way."

"You're right, but I cannot help it."

A wave of pure heat washed over her, and she jerked away from him. *No. No. No!* This wouldn't do at all. If he insisted on trailing behind her, she couldn't possibly tolerate it. Even if his advice regarding the color of curtains was sound, it was not worth having him close.

What was it about him that could make her forget the past, forget the present...forget herself?

She decided right then and there that she needed to give him the slip. She needed to keep her head, and if the only way she could accomplish all she needed to today was to escape, then she would have to do so.

She smiled sweetly. "Since you have firm opinions, you can help me choose other fabrics and colors for table linens."

Did his lips twitch or was it her imagination? Good. If he thought to drive her to distraction with his attempts to seduce and unnerve her, then she could taunt him in return.

She turned her attention to the counter where the shopkeeper stood. She waved the man over. "Mr. Dunston, we have a large order and will need assistance with our selections."

A heavyset, middle-aged man swiftly approached. No doubt he recognized nobility when he saw it. Nonetheless, Ellie made the introductions. "The Marquess of Deveril is aiding me with my choices today."

If the shopkeeper was surprised to have a marquess in his shop selecting fabrics, he did not show it. "Welcome, my lord." Mr. Dunston looked to Ellie. "Where would you prefer to begin?"

"Curtains. We require many, many of them," Ellie said.

The shopkeeper clapped his hands, and two young assistants, who appeared to be his daughters, appeared from behind tall bolts of fabric to aid them.

Ellie took perverse delight in taking her time with her selections. One of his daughters even brought forth sketches of elegant drawing rooms in colorful watercolors as samples.

"Do you have swatches of each of the curtains shown in these sketches?"

The girl bobbed her head. "Yes, miss."

Swatches and bolts of fabric were laid out on a long table for their perusal. Soon, even Ellie became overwhelmed with the selections. But to her surprise, Hugh displayed patience. He shifted through sketches, swatches, and yards of fabric alongside her and picked out what he thought would work best. She grudgingly admitted he had good taste. They arranged for all the goods to be delivered to the Raven Club.

"I see you in a different light, my lord," Ellie said.

"Oh?"

"I believed you would find shopping distasteful."

"Perhaps it is the company."

Devil.

She waited until Mr. Dunston returned with an armful of additional bolts of cloth before making her move.

"I spotted trimmings in the front of the store. Pardon while I fetch what I am looking for," Ellie said.

No one paid her attention. She hurried to the front of the store and, without a word, motioned to Alice to follow. Reaching up, Ellie held the little bell above the door, opened it, and they slipped outside.

Once they were on the street, Ellie took Alice's arm and swiftly walked away. They passed three stores, a haberdasher, a furrier, and a tailor before Alice spoke.

"You realize the marquess will be angry."

Ellie didn't slow her step. "If I get everything done, then it will be worth his ire. Besides, he deserves it."

"Hmm. He doesn't strike me as a man who will easily let

you have your way." Alice's longer strides kept up with Ellie's quick pace.

"It is of no consequence." Her destination was two blocks away, and despite her bold words, she felt an urgency to put as much distance between her and the draper before Hugh even realized she was no longer in the shop.

"Pardon my frankness, miss, but I see the way the marquess looks at you. I do believe you will have more to contend with than you believe."

Ellie let out an unladylike snort. "You are mistaken. The marquess only wants the club."

"I don't believe so. I've been widowed, miss. I know something of men," Alice argued. "His lordship is enamored of you."

Ellie scowled as she walked. She couldn't contend with Alice's comments, not now, not when she had more pressing matters.

"Hurry. We're here." Ellie spotted the furniture maker's wooden sign swinging on its hinges in the slight breeze. Alice opened the door.

With one last glimpse at the street for any sign of Hugh, Ellie swept inside.

• • •

She'd given him the slip.

Hugh had suspected something was amiss. Ellie had a tell—a tiny twitch of her lips when she lied. She'd had it ever since he'd known her. He'd recognized it years ago at a garden party when she'd told her family she'd seen a friend and wanted to stroll the gardens with her. Except there was no friend. Ellie had met Hugh in the gardens, and they'd shared a sweet kiss inside a fragrant maze.

What happened to the innocent girl of his youth?

Ellie had always been intelligent, but now she was bold. Feisty enough to abandon him in a draper's shop. He wished he could have seen her grow from a bookish girl into a fiery woman. He mourned the loss.

He was surrounded by bolts of fabric with an overeager shopkeeper and his assistants. He would laugh at his predicament if he weren't furious.

Ellie couldn't evade him that easily. He felt a heightened anticipation and eagerness he'd lacked for a long, long time. She was a refreshing change since his return from the military. His last mistress, an actress at Drury Lane, had wanted more, and he wasn't interested. But Ellie was different. A challenge. A worthy opponent, not in the ring but in a battle of wits. And Hugh liked nothing better.

If Ellie thought she could fool him, she had met her match.

Chapter Five

A tall, thin shopkeeper with a head of gray hair and a white walrus mustache stood behind the counter. A piece of wood was clamped in a vice, and he used a plane to shave off curls of wood. A pipe rested between his lips, and the scent of spiced tobacco lingered in the shop. She wondered what the piece of wood would become.

"Hello, Mr. Weber," Ellie said.

The man lowered his pipe. His brow furrowed as his gaze focused on Ellie, then he smiled, revealing brown, crooked teeth. "It is delightful to see you, my lady. How is your brother, Lord Castleton?"

The shopkeeper was also the skilled tradesman who had made custom gambling tables for Ian in the past.

"Well. He and the countess are expecting their first child."

"Wonderful." He set his tool on a bench and rubbed his hands on his leather apron. "How can I be of assistance?"

"Lord Castleton will soon require additional gambling tables." It wasn't exactly true. Ellie required them for the ladies' gambling room, but she saw no need to clarify the difference. "But at the present, we need other items. A settee, a number of chairs, and a four-poster bed."

"I'll need to begin work on the gaming tables. Meanwhile, I have furnishings in the back room," Mr. Weber said. "As for a four-poster, you are fortunate. A customer requested one, then never returned to claim it. It is also in the back. Please feel free to peruse the items."

"Thank you."

Once again, Alice stayed in the front of the shop as Ellie made her way to the back room. The large storage space was crammed with rows of furniture the tradesman had made. Ellie inspected chairs with clawed feet; a chaise; a sofa made of mahogany and upholstered with bolster cushions, which could comfortably seat three; walnut and oak side tables with slim legs; and even a music stand. The four-poster was in the far corner. The frame was made of lovely rosewood and was sturdy. A mattress would have to be purchased separately.

Ellie's requirements were simple. She sought a comfortable place for repose while Violet Lasher arranged for a lady to disappear into the countryside—far away from her abusive husband or male family member.

Violet's contacts were vast, and Ellie marveled at the courtesan's ability to alter a lady's appearance and hide her away forever. Violet did not just cut a lady's hair with shears and clothe her differently. Violet transformed them. Hair dyes, cosmetics, and clothing all came into play. Ellie's efforts could not succeed without Violet.

Ellie tallied the items she required in her mind just as raised voices sounded from the front of the shop.

A very distinctive male voice.

Oh no. She had little time to grab her reticule when Hugh Vere burst into the room. Alice was right behind him.

"I tried to stop him, my lady," Alice said, her expression

pained.

Ellie struggled to calm her racing heart. "It's fine, Alice."

Mr. Weber appeared in the doorway. "Is all well?"

"Of course," Ellie said, her mind quickly coming up with an excuse. "The marquess is a friend. He offered to drive us home in his carriage."

Mr. Weber's expression eased. "Is the bed to your liking, my lady? I can arrange to have it delivered straightaway."

Her stomach tilted at the mention of the bed in front of Hugh. She knew it would unleash a slew of questions from him, but she had little choice. She needed the bed for her private chamber. "Yes, please arrange for it," she said to the shopkeeper.

"A bed?" Hugh asked.

Ellie's expression strained, but she kept her smile. "Alice's elderly aunt has come to live with her, and Alice requires a new bed. Isn't that correct, Alice?"

Alice paled, her skin turning the color of old bone, but she caught on quickly and nodded in agreement. "Aunt Henrietta is unwell."

"I'm sorry to hear that, miss," Mr. Weber said.

"Oh, yes. A horrible case of gout," Alice said. She took the shopkeeper's arm, glanced at Ellie, then steered the shopkeeper away, all the while chattering about her aunt's "condition." Ellie was left alone with Hugh in the back room.

She attempted to sweep by him, but he was quick to grasp her arm. "Not so fast. I did not appreciate being abandoned in a draper's shop."

"You asked to accompany me. You did not say everywhere. Besides, you were getting along marvelously with the draper."

He shook his head. "I suspected subterfuge."

"Oh?"

"You have a tell."

"A tell?"

"Your lips twitch. Right here." He stepped close and grazed a spot by her mouth with his finger. She tensed. Her lips tingled from the light touch. She wanted him to touch her mouth, and even more ridiculous, she wanted to lick his finger.

Instead, she took a breath and glared at him. "No one has ever mentioned a twitch before."

"Perhaps they weren't looking at your lips as closely as I have."

Now he was taunting her. Teasing her in the maddening way only he could. "I won't apologize for slipping away," she said.

"I didn't expect it."

"Hmm."

"Why do you need a bed in the club?"

Her mind spun at his change in topic. He was smooth, she'd give him that much. "I don't. Remember, Alice needs it for her sick—"

He shot her a disbelieving look. "You don't expect me to believe that story, do you? Tell me why you need a bed."

How much to tell? She instinctively knew she could not fool him with another lie. She could be truthful, but not confess *everything*. "Fine," she said. "There is a separate room adjacent to the women's gambling room where I intend to keep the bed. Women may get tired and need to rest in the ladies' gambling room."

"Rest? I thought the intended goal is for them to empty their reticules at the tables."

"Ladies have different needs from men. They seek excitement at the tables, but they also like to talk and... maybe rest. From my observation, men do not share this preference."

A look of smug male acknowledgment crossed his

features. "By briefly rest, do you mean entertain a lover?"

Of course he would reach such a conclusion. He was a man, after all. She thought of her options, then decided it couldn't hurt for him to believe this. It might deter further questions.

She shrugged a shoulder. "I will not protest if a lady chooses to rest alone or with another."

To her surprise, a flash of anger crossed his face. "Oh? And what would your brother say? Is he aware of his sister's plans to improve the profitability of the club by turning it into a brothel?"

He would think the worst. Her nervousness at Hugh's inquiries suddenly veered into anger. "Why do you keep bringing up my brother? It is becoming tiresome."

"You need reminding."

"If you must know, I do not intend to turn it into a house of ill repute. No money shall exchange hands. Only if a lady is fatigued or drinks a bit too much wine, then she shall make use of the bed. The women's room will be for gambling only."

He studied her, his eyes traveling over her face as if he could reach inside her head and read her thoughts. "Then I need not fear of your plans," he said.

His arrogant tone proclaimed that her efforts could never compete with his, and that he would undoubtedly be the victor. She glared. "You should. I still intend to win the club."

His eyebrow rose. "You do not yet know all of my plans."

"I'm still confident that I'll win."

He cocked his head to the side and continued to watch her in an intense way that made heat run down her spine. "I wish I had been there to see it."

She blinked. He had a maddening way of continuing to change the topic. "See what?"

"See you grow into the woman you are today. You were always sweet and lovely, especially your enchanting freckles."

Enchanting freckles? She made a mental note to vigorously rub more of the expensive depilatory she'd purchased on the bridge of her nose tonight.

"But now you are temptation itself."

Temptation? She would not succumb to such blatant masculine nonsense. He might be used to women fawning over him, but she was not one of them. *Liar.* Then why did his words make her heart beat fast? She must never let him know.

"Don't be ridiculous," she said. "Your charm will not work on me."

He arched a dark eyebrow. "I'm wounded."

"It's true."

"Then you won't worry if I try."

Her heart slammed against her chest. "Try what?"

"This." He lowered his head and brushed his lips against hers.

She froze, afraid to breathe. He touched her with nothing but his lips, but it was as if iron bands held her in place. He brushed against her mouth once…twice. Featherweight kisses that surprised her with their gentleness, but no less seductive.

"I've wanted to kiss you properly since our ringside kiss." His lips continued to brush against hers as he spoke.

He had?

He kissed the corners of her mouth, then his tongue licked the seam of her lips. The velvet warmth of his kiss was mesmerizing, and her lips parted of their own volition. She took a step forward, and her tongue met his, tentative at first, then more eagerly. A low growl came from his chest as he pulled her to him and deepened the kiss.

Oh my. It was everything she'd ever remembered and so much more.

He was all hard muscle and sinew, so different from her soft form. His kiss was like tasting a bit of the sky and the scorching sun. Heat engulfed her, traveling down her spine and warming her limbs. She heard a mewling noise. Shocked, she realized it had come from her.

More.

Her brain seemed to freeze, and her body, her treacherous body, pulsed in awareness of the man. *Danger*, her mind warned. *Delicious*, her body answered. It was an infuriatingly arousing combination. This was Hugh. The boy who had captured her heart and crushed it in one moment in a stranger's gardens. The man who came crashing back into her life and challenged her for all she'd ever wanted.

She wanted his kiss to last and to end. It was torturous.

Even more maddening, *he* was the one to break the kiss.

"Ellie," he said simply as he gazed down at her.

The mention of her name brought her to her senses. "That was a mistake."

"It didn't feel like a mistake to me." His breath was warm and sweet against her lips. "I was wrong to treat you as I did years ago. Can you forget the past?"

It was as if he dumped a bucket of ice water on her head. "Forget the past? I caught you kissing Isabella West in the gardens of a ball. The same gardens where we were to meet."

A flash of remorse crossed his features. "That was years ago."

"Nothing has changed," she snapped.

"What if I told you it has for me?"

She felt an overwhelming need to either kiss him or slap him. Fortunately, the latter impulse won out. Her slap echoed in the storage room.

She froze in surprise at what she'd done. She'd never exhibited violence before, never struck a person.

"I'll allow that once."

His tone sent a chill down her spine. It had been years since she'd known him. He'd gone off to fight in the military. He was, in essence, a stranger. And she'd slapped him.

She didn't fear physical harm, but the warning in his eyes resonated all the same.

"Do not think I am the same foolish girl," she said.

He clenched his jaw and touched his cheek. She'd left a red mark. "I never thought you foolish."

"Then you must think me an idiot now to fall for your weak attempts at seduction."

"Weak? You kissed me back quite enthusiastically."

His response angered her, and she grasped at the emotion, let it consume her and replace the weakness she'd experienced at his kiss. "You want the club. I now realize that you will use any means to get it."

His brows drew downward. "Our kiss had nothing to do with the club."

She wasn't sure. He was a handsome man who could easily charm and seduce. She'd known women foolish enough to ruin their reputations and fall prey to scoundrels. She never thought she was weak enough to be one of them. But now she understood the powerful allure of a skilled seducer.

She was saved from having to come up with an answer when Alice appeared in the doorway and cleared her throat. "Your carriage is waiting outside, my lord."

Relief swept through Ellie. She didn't want to address his response regarding their kiss. She couldn't make it to the carriage fast enough. To her further dismay, Hugh captured her arm and was right by her side.

Chapter Six

The next day, Ellie was determined to keep her mind on her work and forget Hugh's kiss. That didn't mean, however, that she would ignore him. If he had discerned her plans for the club, then she had better discover his.

Locating Hugh in the boxing room in the back of the club was not difficult. She expected to find the marquess speaking with Brooks about how best to add another ring or more space for standing spectators to watch the fights. Instead, she found Hugh shirtless and performing some kind of exercise. A steel bar was mounted between two walls in an alcove, and he was pulling himself up to it with his arms, then slowly lowering himself down inch by inch. Then he repeated the effort.

She halted in mid-stride at the sight. His biceps flexed with each movement. His shoulders strained.

Heavens. There were muscles *everywhere*.

He hadn't yet noticed her. She was standing to the side of the roped ring, and the soft leather soles of her slippers were silent on the hardwood floor. Memories of their kiss returned in a rush of emotion, and wings fluttered in her belly as she watched him. She'd only touched him through his clothing, and still his heat and strength had left an impression on her. What would it feel like to run her fingers across all that bronzed skin? All night she'd forced herself to forget his kiss, but now, standing here watching him, she realized her efforts had been in vain.

She cleared her throat. Loudly.

His green gaze snapped to hers, but to her chagrin, he persisted in his activity.

He strained to pull himself up, then slowly lowered himself.

"Have you come to spy on me?" he asked, his voice gruff from his exertions.

Despite her resolve to remain distant, her throat was suddenly dry. "Spy? You were the one who insisted on watching me. I decided to do the same."

"You snuck away and left me in the draper's shop with an overzealous shopkeeper."

Up. Then down again.

A rivulet of sweat rolled down his chest, traveled down his abdomen, slipped through a sprinkling of dark hair, and disappeared into the waistband of his trousers.

Indecent. Ungentlemanly.

"You cannot blame me. I don't trust you," she said.

"You made that perfectly clear."

Was he still furious at her for leaving him in the draper's shop? Was he trying to intimidate her with these calisthenics?

She cleared her throat. "Well? What are your plans to win against me? All I see is…this," she said, sweeping her hand toward him.

He released the bar to land on the balls of his feet. Somehow the movement was graceful and predatory at the same time and reminded her of a jungle cat. His eyes met hers, his chest slightly rising and falling from his efforts.

Had she wanted his attention? He was giving it to her now. She fought the urge to back up a step.

He reached for a cloth and wiped the sweat from his brow, then his chest. Her gaze followed. It was impossible not to watch him.

He possessed a perfect male form. She didn't remember him like this. He'd been a lean youth when he'd held her all those years ago. But now, he was… He was huge. It was how she'd attempted to describe him to her sister. No words could do him justice. He should put a shirt on.

He *had* to put a shirt on.

"You want to know?" he asked.

Her eyes snapped back to his, and her cheeks felt flushed. She was suddenly over-warm, and her lungs strained in her corset. "Know what?" Had he noticed her staring? How could he not have? How humiliating.

One dark eyebrow arched, as if he knew her wicked thoughts and was perfectly capable of satisfying each one. "Do you want to know what I have planned?"

"Yes…yes, of course. That's why I'm here." Certainly not to watch him. Never that. "Perhaps you should dress before we converse."

His lips twitched, but thankfully he made no comment. He tossed the towel on the roped ring and reached for a shirt he'd thrown across a wooden chair. His slipped it over his head. The cotton had been rolled up and revealed his forearms. Without a cravat, she could still see the corded muscles of his neck and the sprinkling of hair on his chest.

She'd asked him to don a shirt, but that did little to cease her racing heart. She dragged her gaze away.

"I intend to increase the number of boxing matches by adding more rings," he said, pointing to the empty space in the back of the cavernous room. "Two matches can occur back to back, or even at the same time."

"I see." Her mind started to calculate all the extra money the matches would bring into the club. It was a good plan, but—

"I also intend to add croupiers."

She frowned. "You plan to add gambling tables in the boxing room?"

"No. Just the croupiers. I want them walking around and taking bets before, during, and between fights. The way it stands now, there is only one man in the corner of the room taking wagers. The room is packed during the fights, so no one can even reach him. But if I add more croupiers and have them walking through the crowd, I believe I can triple the revenue."

She was impressed. It wasn't something she'd thought of. She was handling the books more and more, especially since Grace was nearing her birth, and Ellie knew precisely how lucrative the fights could be.

"And as I already mentioned, I plan to invite the champions to attend. I know Gentleman John Jackson has his own boxing salon, but I hope to have him as a guest or a referee. There won't be an empty spectators' seat or a place to stand."

His plan had serious merit. He was right. Champions did have their own salons, but with an invitation from the Marquess of Deveril to the Raven Club, it just might be enough to entice them to attend. If one champion came, then the others would feel compelled to show as well.

For the first time, Ellie experienced a true nervousness that Hugh Vere might win the club. No matter how certain she was that a ladies' gambling room could bring in money, Hugh's endeavor could easily rival her plans.

No. Too much was at stake. Women were depending on her. Violet Lasher was as well.

"I see," was all she managed to say. She experienced a

burning need to get back to the unfinished women's gambling room, to ensure her plan was more successful than his. "Now if you'll excuse me, I have work to accomplish."

He shrugged, then picked up what looked like a short iron bar. He raised and lowered it in his hand. With his rolled-up shirtsleeves, the muscles in his forearms bulged—different muscles from the ones she'd seen when he had been pulling himself up from the mounted bar. She wanted to reach out and feel if his forearm was as hard as it looked. His masculine form was so different from hers. It was fascinating.

She was aware of the harsh, uneven rhythm of her own breathing, and she hadn't lifted a finger. She blinked and turned to leave, then halted. Before she departed, she realized that she had one more item to address. "I apologize for striking you. It is unlike me."

He lowered the weight but did not release it. "Why did you?" he asked.

She struggled with the words. "You said things. Unnerving things that reminded me of the past."

His intense gaze met hers and tugged at the deepest corner of her heart. "Would it help if I told you kissing Isabelle that night in the gardens was the worst thing I've ever done? I did not enjoy it."

Then why did you?

She wanted to scream the question. Instead, she folded her hands in front of her. His confession was not the reason for her apology. She didn't want to delve into the past. She'd spent years wondering why he'd done what he had, and she refused to return to that dark place now.

She was stronger. Older.

"It no longer matters," she said. "All that concerns me now is the Raven Club." That much was true. They were not meant to be together. In hindsight, it was better that she'd caught Hugh with Isabelle that day. If they'd married, Hugh would have not only broken her heart, but *her*, when he sought out another as he most assuredly would have done.

A shadow flickered in his eyes. "Perhaps you're right and it no longer matters. But as for the club, I still find your motivations for wanting the establishment surprising."

"I can say the same for you. You are no longer a second son but a marquess," she countered.

"The title is not all I want to be. I want to do something with my life other than to manage my stewards and take my seat in the House of Lords. I want *more*."

She raised her chin. "So do I."

He walked close, until they were only a few feet apart, and her heart jumped. "The young Ellie I knew loved books. She wanted to marry and have exactly four children—two boys and two girls. She wanted a large library complete with Shakespeare's plays and Grimms' fairy tales. She wanted a garden. She wanted to laugh every day. I've only heard you laugh once since."

Damn him. Once again, he was confusing her by bringing up tender memories of the past. Memories that weren't true, but veiled in lies and betrayal. "You ruined that girl. Crushed her heart."

His green eyes blazed, not with fury, but with an intensity that made her chest tighten. "Then that is my greatest regret. I want to see you laugh again. Is there something I can do?"

Sorrow raged with anger, and her temper rose in response. "Yes. You can leave. I'll surely laugh after I beat you and win the Raven."

She turned on her heel and strode out.

• • •

"I've convinced Lady Willoughby to come to the Raven," Olivia said.

"How?" Ellie asked.

The sisters were on the terrace enjoying a luncheon at home. It was a lovely afternoon and not a cloud marred the sky. Large terra-cotta pots with fragrant blooms scented the air, and the girls sipped glasses of lemonade.

A frown marred Olivia's brow, and she lowered her glass. "I saw Samantha yesterday afternoon. We were to have afternoon tea at her home. She sent a note to cancel at the last minute, but I had a dreadful sense of foreboding and showed up on her doorstep and claimed I never received her note. I acted quite unladylike and pushed my way past her butler and into her home."

Ellie rolled her eyes. "You, unladylike? I cannot imagine." Olivia could be quite persistent when she wanted something.

"Yes, well...before the butler or anyone else could stop me, I hurried up the grand staircase and burst into Samantha's bedchamber."

"You're lucky the baron wasn't home!"

"I was willing to take the risk. I also quickly realized he was not in residence because I never heard his booming voice."

Ellie let out a held-in breath. "I take it Lady Willoughby was home."

Olivia's expression grew hard. "There were bruises everywhere. Samantha claimed she tripped on the front step as she was returning home the prior evening. It was a ridiculous lie."

Silence stretched between them for seconds.

"How did you convince her to come to the Raven Club? I thought she feared the baron discovering her whereabouts?"

"She does. But this last beating was worse than the others. He blames her for not conceiving an heir and promised to continue until she produces a male child."

Ellie's insides twisted in disgust. She already despised

the viscount, and she'd only made his acquaintance once at a ball. "When can I expect Lady Willoughby?"

"Tomorrow evening."

"Will you accompany her?"

"No. Even if we are both masked, Samantha fears others will recognize her if we are seen together."

Ellie nodded. "I will seek her out. You have done the right thing, Olivia."

Olivia bit her bottom lip. "I hope so. But convincing her to leave her husband will not be easy."

"It never is."

• • •

"I need your help, Brooks," Ellie said. "Furnishings are to be delivered today for my ladies' gambling room. I need assistance overseeing everything, and most likely, some of the heavier items will have to be moved."

She'd found Brooks in the club's kitchens talking with Cook and finishing off a platter of cold roast beef and cheese.

Brooks scraped back his chair and stood. "I am at your service, my lady."

These days, her brother was at home with Grace more often than he was at the club, so he couldn't help. Grace's time was drawing near, and her brother was reluctant to leave his wife's side.

The only other male who was strong enough to help was Hugh, and she refused to ask him.

Brooks had never expressed his opinion as to whether he preferred Ellie or the Marquess of Deveril to win the Raven. The man was intelligent and loyal to her brother. As a result, she was hesitant to confess everything to him. But she was also wise enough to know that Brooks might learn the truth on his own. The man walked the club floor each night and spoke with the servants. He may be fine with a private room for the women to gamble, but when it came to the hidden room, she had to tell him before he discovered it and questioned her. As with Hugh, she would not tell Brooks the whole truth.

"Some of the items require secrecy."

Brooks's gaze snapped to hers. "Such as?"

"It's best if I show you."

A half hour later, the items arrived, and the furnishings were carried inside—a settee, numerous chairs, end tables with clawed feet, and a chest of drawers.

The four-poster bed arrived last and needed to be assembled. She directed Brooks and the burly men to the private room.

Brooks touched her sleeve. "A bed, my lady?"

She shrugged and stepped away. If she could have arranged everything without Brooks's knowledge, she would have. "I thought it would be nice for the ladies to have a place to rest if needed."

His brow drew downward. "You mean a place to spend the night with a lover?"

"No!" Why did men immediately leap to the same conclusion—that she intended to turn the club into a brothel?

"Ah, I see. You intend a lady to spend an evening away from a spouse?"

He was much closer now. Her fingers tangled in her skirts. She didn't know if the truth was more damaging than his initial assumption. Looking into his black eyes, she knew it was best if he was on her side.

"You know?"

"I do."

"You will not tell the marquess?"

"You're worried about Deveril? What about your brother?"

This was a tricky question, and she was unsure how

to answer. "It's only for one night. Nothing more. Ian will understand. Grace will make him." She wasn't sure about this. In fact, she doubted her brother would support her, but it was critical that Brooks didn't see or hear the wavering in her voice.

Besides, Ellie considered this Ian's doing. Unbeknownst to her brother, Ian had ignited this passion in Ellie. He had helped Ellie's friend, Mary, and allowed her safe refuge in the Raven Club. He'd also delighted in denying her husband membership to the Raven. If only it had been enough.

Brooks stared down at her. Whether he knew the truth, he stayed silent. Several tense seconds of silence passed, and Ellie feared he could hear the pounding of her heart. At last, his fierce expression softened, and his lips curled into what was the closest thing Ellie had seen to a smile from him. "How can I help?"

"I need help arranging the furnishings, especially the four-poster bed."

Brooks took off his jacket and tossed it on a chair. "Anything else?"

She let out a breath. "Please keep it from the marquess."

Chapter Seven

What the hell is going on?

Hugh leaned from behind a corridor and watched as Brooks and Ellie emerged from the paneled room. Brooks carried his jacket, waistcoat, and cravat.

Hugh had seen workmen deliver furnishings to Ellie's private gambling room. But they had departed a half hour ago. So what was Brooks doing inside with Ellie? And why was the man partially undressed?

An unfamiliar knot tightened in his chest. Ellie couldn't possibly be having an illicit liaison with the burly man, could she?

Hugh had never understood why Ellie never married. She was lovely, and she came from a wealthy, titled family. If rumor stood true, she had a large enough dowry to attract a flock of the *beau monde's* bachelors.

Hugh's mother had insisted Ellie's family had been tainted with scandal. But other men wouldn't mind, not if they had Ellie to warm their bed each night along with her dowry.

Was that what Brooks was hoping for?

The knot in his chest began to burn.

Christ! Was he jealous? Since returning to London, he'd had his share of bed sport and had never experienced jealousy over a woman. And he hadn't even bedded Ellie.

Not that he didn't want to.

He knew she wasn't immune to him, either. He'd seen the way she'd raptly watched him when she'd interrupted his calisthenics in the boxing room. Her gaze had licked over his skin like flame, her breasts had risen and fallen above her bodice, and it had taken every ounce of self-control not to pull her into his arms and kiss her senseless. When he'd kissed her in the shopkeeper's back room, the heated moment had only served to whet his appetite, his fierce desire for her.

Brooks lowered his head to Ellie's ear to speak, and she smiled and laughed. He'd only heard her laugh once since his return, and it had been brief.

The sound vibrated through him, leaving an empty hole in his chest. She used to often laugh for *him*.

Now she was gifting another with the pleasure.

Damnation.

He wanted her back. Her laugh, her smile, her intelligent conversation, her tempting kisses, her *everything*.

What had started as a competition for the club had turned into much, much more. The problem was she seemed excited by the competition and was determined not to lose.

And here he was...her adversary, a man intent on protecting her by besting her.

• • •

Ellie stood at the window in the upstairs office overlooking the casino floor. Every table was crowded that night, even the macao and loo tables, which were usually second to the faro, hazard, and roulette tables.

A boxing match was scheduled for the evening, and more gamblers would rush to the casino floor immediately afterward to wager their winnings. Hugh was not within sight, and she assumed he was overseeing the pugilists before they stepped into the ring.

Good. It would allow her time to conduct her business without his infernal interference.

Ellie spotted Lady Willoughby as soon as she set foot inside. Even with her simple blue half mask, Ellie recognized the pale blond hair and willowy figure. Brooks was standing by the door and allowed the lady to pass. Ellie had given Olivia a secret word in order to gain admittance, and Olivia in turn had conveyed it to Lady Willoughby.

Ellie waited a half hour before slipping on her peacock mask and leaving the room. She did not want to draw unwanted attention to the lady straightaway.

She approached Lady Willoughby by the roulette table just as the croupier cried out, "Twenty-eight black. The lady wins!"

Patrons shouted in dismay as the croupier collected their losses. Ellie slipped to the woman's right. "Luck is with you tonight."

Lady Willoughby turned. "Luck hasn't been with me in a long time."

The mask didn't cover the woman's entire face, and Ellie could see a new bruise on her right cheekbone. She had attempted to hide all the bruises with face powder, but up close, Ellie could tell. It had only been a few days since Olivia had told her of Lady Willoughby's plight. Had her husband beaten her again?

Ellie's fists clenched at her sides. She took a breath, counted to ten, and forced her fingers to relax. The last thing she wanted to do was frighten the woman upon their first meeting.

"I am Olivia's sister," Ellie said.

The lady nodded once. "She told me to expect you."

"Please collect your winnings and follow me."

Ellie led the lady, not to the stairs leading to the office, but around a corner to the paneled wall. Ellie reached for the latch, and the door swung open.

Lady Willoughby's step faltered. "Is it safe?"

"Yes."

She followed Ellie inside. The room was almost complete. Furnishings had been delivered, the room painted, and blue curtains hung, but there hadn't been time to add additional gambling tables. Only the single roulette table stood in the center of the large room.

Lady Willoughby walked farther inside. Her gloved fingertips traced the back of a settee. "What is this place?"

"It will be a women's gambling room. A place where men are not permitted. The only males who will cross the threshold will be liveried servers."

"Truly? A place without men? How lovely." Lady Willoughby stopped by the roulette table and spun the wheel. Without a little white ball, it sounded different as it spun and came to a stop.

Ellie could only imagine the lady's thoughts regarding a place without men. Safety. A haven. A brief escape from her hellish existence living with a brute.

"I admit to being pleasantly surprised. But do you believe you will have sufficient business to justify a women's room?" Lady Willoughby asked.

Ellie chuckled. "Have you noticed how many ladies are on the casino floor this evening?"

"Yes, I have. Some are unmasked. They are not all ladies." Lady Willoughby touched her own mask, a simple deep blue one that matched her dress.

"True."

"You allow them entrance?"

"They are wealthy women. Widows or wives of merchants. The Raven Club is not Almack's. There are no discerning patronesses who hand out vouchers."

"Thank heavens for that," the lady said.

So far, everything was progressing as planned. Lady Willoughby had come to the club. She had followed Ellie into the private room and seemed excited at the prospect of a women's space. Could Ellie convince her to take one more step?

"Come. There is more to see," Ellie said.

Lady Willoughby followed as Ellie led her to the back of the room. Ellie pressed another latch, this one smaller, and a hidden door in the panel swung open quietly.

Samantha Willoughby's lips parted. "Another hidden room?"

Ellie didn't answer but stepped inside to reveal the smaller room. The lady halted, her brown eyes wide behind her mask. "A bedchamber?"

The room had been painted and decorated in cream colors. Brooks had come through, and the four-poster bed had been assembled and a feathered mattress delivered. A peach coverlet gave the room a warm feel. A chest of drawers sat in the corner. A lace runner and porcelain bowl for washing rested upon the chest.

"It's a place to stay. Safe and hidden," Ellie said.

"From whom?

"From men."

Lady Willoughby stiffened, and she bit her bottom lip. "Olivia told you everything, didn't she?"

There was no sense lying, not now. "She did."

Slowly, Lady Willoughby removed her mask. She did not make eye contact with Ellie, but Ellie saw enough.

She cringed in horror. The lady's husband *had* beaten her more. Much more from what Olivia had described. His handiwork showed in the dark purple bruising around both of his wife's eyes. She looked worse than the pugilists in the boxing ring. Ellie felt a nauseating sickness and swallowed hard.

"When did he do this to you?" Ellie said, her voice a hoarse whisper.

Lady Willoughby shook her head, still refusing to look directly at her. "I'm clumsy and took a tumble down the stairs."

"There is no need to lie. I will not whisper a word."

"Like your sister?" the lady asked, a note of censure in her strained voice.

Ellie was not put off. "Olivia is concerned for you."

The lady's chin stiffened. "There is no need for anyone's concern. I am fine."

"Are you? What if you conceive a child? Would you want a babe to be just as 'fine' in your husband's care?"

Lady Willoughby took a quick breath. "How dare you!"

"I dare because you do not speak the truth."

The woman raised a trembling hand to one of her blackened eyes, and a cry escaped her lips—a sad, desperate sound like that of a wounded and cornered animal. It tugged at Ellie's heart, and it took all her effort not to reach out and cradle the woman in her arms.

"What is the use in subterfuge? You know."

Ellie dared to step forward to touch her arm. She feared the lady would bolt, like a frightened deer. "There is help. We have helped others."

"How?" Samantha's voice trembled.

"You must be willing to do what is necessary."

"Harm my husband?"

Ellie's lips thinned. "That wasn't what I had in mind,

although I can understand how you would feel that way."

"I don't! What else is there?"

"Your departure from London can be arranged. A new start."

"You mean for me to disappear?"

"In a sense. You must be willing to assume a new name and flee. I understand it is a difficult choice. You will lose your title as a lady, along with the wealth it provides."

Lady Willoughby shook her head. "I don't know."

Ellie pressed on; she knew she had to. If her gut instinct was right, then the woman's situation was dire. Even Olivia had not known all of her friend's circumstances. "Who or what keeps you here in London?"

"My mother and father. They would be ashamed if I…if I left the baron." Her voice was small, broken.

"Do they know how he shows his affection?"

"I tried to tell them. They suggested I try harder to please my husband, and that my plight is the result of his displeasure."

Anger blossomed in Ellie's chest. How could the woman's parents be so cruel? Their refusal to aid their daughter was as unconscionable as the baron's physical beatings in Ellie's opinion. She knew divorce was scandalous, but if a husband took his fists to Ellie, she knew without a doubt, Ian would protect her from an abusive spouse. "And you? How do you feel about your husband?"

For the first time, Lady Willoughby met Ellie's gaze straight on. "I *hate* him."

· · ·

Something was going on in the hidden room.

Brooks entered and left twice. The large man tugged on his collar, then a few minutes later, the paneled door swung open and Ellie exited. Whatever they were doing inside had continued.

Damn it.

He was going to find out the truth.

Hugh knew the four-poster bed had already been delivered. He'd seen workmen carry it in piece by piece along with a rolled Oriental carpet. He still couldn't understand why Ellie wanted a bed in the ladies' gambling room.

He'd wanted to believe her excuse that a lady might need to rest, but then common sense had taken hold. That, and he'd seen Brooks and Ellie enter and leave the room together more than once.

He was truly a fool.

He might have no right where Ellie was concerned, but he refused to allow her to have a liaison with Brooks.

Not when she'd kissed Hugh with such passion. Not when she'd made those little mewling noises that had kept him up at night thinking of her.

How could she forget their shared kiss so easily? Christ, he'd thought of little else over the past two days.

Perhaps it was his vanity. He'd never cared about a lover leaving his bed for another. He'd never entertained them for more than a brief time before moving on.

But this was different.

She was different.

Hugh waited for Brooks to walk away before making his move. Ellie remained in the room.

Perfect.

Hugh pressed the latch, opened the door, and slipped inside. He found her bent over the roulette table, reading a sheaf of papers. She straightened when she spotted him.

"What are you doing in here?" she asked.

"I was looking for you. You weren't in the office, the boxing room, or strolling the casino floor."

"I wasn't aware I was supposed to keep you apprised of my whereabouts," Ellie said.

"I spotted you enter this room. I also saw Brooks enter and leave here. Twice."

"So?"

"What's going on between you two?"

"Careful," she said, her voice a tantalizing whisper. "You sound jealous."

He guffawed. It sounded strained to his own ears. "Jealous? I've never experienced the emotion."

"Thank you for reminding me of your ways. Now, I've told you of my plans with this room. Brooks is merely helping me carrying out my vision."

"Your vision? I hope by that you mean moving furnishings and heavy carpets."

"Precisely."

He glanced around the room, noting the furnishings and curtains. A settee and a table and chairs were situated around the perimeter of the room. A large Oriental carpet covered the hardwood floors. Blue silk drapes artfully framed the walls in a luxurious display. A bed was notably absent, but then he recalled Ellie telling him it was to be in a separate chamber.

"You chose the blue silk," he said.

She shrugged one delicate shoulder. "I told you in the draper's that I agreed with your suggestion. Now why are you really here? I find it hard to believe you burst inside this room to see if I have taken a lover. I think you are here to see how far I've come? To see what I still require?"

He should say yes. His motivations for seeking her out today should have to do with their rivalry. But it was furthest from the truth. He'd burst in here not to observe how much she'd accomplished, but to confirm she was not with another man. That there was nothing going on between her and

Brooks.

Because he couldn't stop thinking about her. "Do you ever recall our kiss?"

She paled a shade, bringing the freckles on her nose to higher contrast. Damn if he didn't find it charming.

"I said it was a mistake and to forget what occurred," she said.

"Forget it? Impossible. I've thought of little else."

She planted her hands on her hips. "You cannot confront me and accuse me of having a secret amorous affair with the club's head guard and then talk about our shared kiss like you want to repeat it. You had more romantic flair years ago."

He wanted to haul her to his chest and show her just how much flair he had, how much he wanted to kiss and lick her until she cried out in pleasure. She was driving him to distraction. Perhaps that was her game? It had been five years. She was a lovely woman in her prime. She might not have been intimate with Brooks, but what if she wasn't innocent and had taken other lovers?

He couldn't blame her, yet...yet the idea of any other male touching her made his gut clench.

"Rest assured if I were trying to seduce you, you would know it."

She leaned away from the table, the simple movement smooth and enticing. The sliver of skin at her collarbone was like fine porcelain, and he wanted to press his lips against the sensitive pulse at her neck to taste the tantalizing skin.

She met his gaze, her blue eyes watchful, and he wondered if she had the slightest inkling of his thoughts. "Hmm. What else do you want then? To kiss me again?"

He did. Desperately. But he also knew she was challenging him, and he wouldn't fall for her ploy. If he said yes, if he made the slightest move, she'd refuse him in a heartbeat.

No, he'd bide his time. Slowly entice her and bring out the

burning sweetness that seemed captive within her.

"If you're finished with me, you should leave," she said.

He wasn't finished with her. Not even close. But he nodded and stepped aside. "As you wish."

He caught her sidelong look. The slightest hesitation and the parting of her lips. She was surprised he hadn't tried to stop her, to kiss her again.

Good. If he was in torment, it was only fair that she suffered, too.

Chapter Eight

Outside the baker's shop stood a boy selling warm rolls to morning passersby from a tray hanging around his neck. Ellie purchased two rolls, then headed for the alleyway between the baker's shop and the Cock and Bull tavern.

Violet's carriage appeared soon after, and Ellie crossed the street to join her inside the conveyance. The courtesan wore a blood-red cloak with a hood, and wisps of blond hair framed her heart-shaped face.

Ellie handed her one of the hot rolls. "Lady Willoughby has agreed."

Violet took a small bite, then nodded. "Good. I will arrange for a conveyance to take her to Kent."

"Kent? I thought you would send her to Scotland, as you did with the other lady."

Violet swallowed before answering. "I cannot send everyone to Scotland. Besides, Lady Willoughby is a difficult matter. Her husband will not stop looking for her."

"So? Eventually, he will cease his efforts when he cannot locate her. He will assume she ran away with a lover."

Violet tapped her lip with a forefinger. "It won't work with the baron. He will never cease searching for his wayward wife. He may even hire investigators to find her. We can never be truly certain of her safety from the man. We have to do more."

"Such as?"

"Fake her death."

Ellie blinked in surprise. They'd never attempted something so dangerous in the past. "How? We've never accomplished such an undertaking."

"An accident."

Ellie's mind spun with possibilities. "It must be believable. Witnesses would be preferable."

"I will think upon it and send a missive to meet with you before the end of the month. Until then, do not whisper a word of our conversation, not even to your sister. Everything must be kept secret."

"Of course. But what about Lady Willoughby?" Ellie asked.

"I'll leave it to your judgement. If she needs time to decide, then she should be told. Meanwhile, continue to invite her to the Raven Club and befriend her."

• • •

The second time Lady Willoughby appeared at the Raven Club, Ellie was waiting for her on the casino floor. It was a busy night, and all the tables were crowded with gamblers hoping to have a streak of luck. The gentlemen were dressed in dark-colored coats and trousers. Beside them, the women looked vivid and colorful in gowns of satins and silks and elaborate spangled and feathered masks. Lady Willoughby was dressed similarly in a green gown, but she was careful not to remain long near any one person. If one looked closely at her, it appeared as if her nerves twitched with a restless energy.

Ellie watched the woman, her own nerves prickling. She wove through the crowd and stopped by one of the macao tables. Careful not to look directly at her, she edged closer. "I'm glad you came."

Lady Willoughby kept her gaze fixed on the players' hands but nodded once. "I thought about what you said."

"And?"

"May we speak in private?"

Ellie turned and walked away, aware that Lady Willoughby followed her. If anyone were watching them, it would appear that they both tired of the game and headed off to seek different entertainment.

Rather than go to the paneled door that led to her unfinished women's gaming room, Ellie decided to take Lady Willoughby elsewhere. Ever since Hugh had burst in and found Ellie alone in the room, she didn't want to risk being caught again. He was observant, and if she was truthful to herself, his presence had disturbed her in too many ways.

Ellie had been certain he'd wanted to kiss her again, but he'd simply left. It's what she'd wanted, wasn't it?

So why did she still feel disgruntled?

She had been so sure her heart was guarded from his charms. After all these years, she'd convinced herself she was immune to him. Her heart might be guarded, but not her treacherous body.

Despite what she'd told him, she *had* relived their kiss. Many times.

Do not think of it!

She had much more pressing things to accomplish, especially tonight.

She forced her thoughts aside and focused on the task at hand. She led Lady Willoughby to the last place Hugh would look tonight. The boxing room in the back of the club. There wasn't a match this evening, and the doors were locked. She'd seen Hugh lingering by the faro tables for most of the night and talking with a group of men. He was distracted, at least for a good amount of time, and wouldn't come here.

Once they were away from the thick of the crowd, Lady Willoughby caught up with Ellie. "Aren't we going to the women's gambling room?"

"Not this time."

They'd reached the tall wooden door. Ellie reached for a key in her pocket, inserted it in the lock, and pushed it open. Lady Willoughby followed her inside. The large room was empty and dimly lit. She could vaguely make out the four corners of the boxing ring.

"It's safe and private here," Ellie said.

Lady Willoughby removed her mask. "I've been thinking quite a bit about what you said when we'd first met. The baron has been ranting incessantly that he wants his heir, and he's been…he's been visiting my bedchamber every night. I dread the evenings. I don't know how much more I can stand." A flush crept over her cheeks, whether in shame or desperation or both, it wasn't clear.

Ellie's breath caught in her throat. She knew many would consider it the baron's right to bed his wife, whether or not it was against her will. But the thought of Lord Willoughby forcing himself upon his young wife made bile rise in her throat.

"Do you believe the baron would search for you if you disappeared from London?" Ellie asked.

Pain flickered in the lady's eyes along with a tired sadness that appeared across her drawn face. "He'd hunt me to his dying day."

Ellie stared at her, letting her anxiety fuel her own resolve for what needed to be done. "Then we have no choice but to fake your death."

Lady Willoughby looked at her in shock. "Fake my death? Good heavens, how?"

Ellie hadn't heard from Violet in days, and she'd rarely reached out to the courtesan in the past. It was not unusual. Violet only contacted her when she had news. Otherwise, it was too risky and could expose not only herself but their working relationship as well.

But Lady Willoughby was desperate to escape her brutish husband. Ellie could see it in her gaze and hear the thread of panic in her voice. She tried not to picture her, trapped in a room with a man twice her size, with nothing to defend herself against his fists and fury.

"I don't know yet, but we will think of a plan," Ellie said.

"It's not possible to—"

Shouts sounded from outside the boxing room. Ellie frowned as she cracked open the door. A large, barrel-shaped man was standing by the entrance arguing with the guard on duty.

Lady Willoughby peered around Ellie's shoulder and gasped. "Oh God! The baron is here."

Ellie's nerves tensed. "Does he know you are here tonight?"

The lady shook her head, her face pale. "I told him I was attending Lady Godfrey's ball. He must have followed me."

The liveried man at the door was no match for the physically larger baron. If only Brooks were here, but it was his evening off.

"Stay here. Let me handle this," Ellie said.

She slipped on her peacock mask and headed for the door. She'd handled disgruntled patrons in the past. The threat of a revoked membership was generally enough to calm their surly disposition after a large loss at one of the tables. She could turn away an angry husband.

As she approached, she sized up the baron. He was a tall, heavyset man. With thinning brown hair, brown eyes, and a bulbous nose, he appeared at least a decade older than his wife. His head rested upon broad shoulders and gave him the appearance that he had no neck.

A trickle of trepidation traveled down Ellie's spine, but she ignored it. There was no time for hesitation or fear. She needed to get the baron out of the club and far away from his wife. "May I be of assistance, my lord?" Ellie said.

Lord Willoughby glared down at her. He reeked of alcohol, cigar smoke, and barely suppressed anger. "I'm looking for my wife."

Ellie schooled her expression and lowered her voice. "Your wife? I know all the ladies here tonight, my lord. She is not present."

"Get out of my way."

Her pulse began to beat erratically at the threat in his deep voice. He made to move past her, but Ellie stepped in front of him and raised a hand. "I insist you leave. You do not have membership here. Only those who have been admitted are allowed inside."

The command lingered, and for a moment Ellie believed it would work, but then his red-rimmed eyes glared down at her with annoyance. "Step aside."

"I said you do not—"

"My wife is here, *dammit*."

The liveried servant stepped in front of Ellie and tried to interfere. "The lady is correct."

Lord Willoughby shoved the guard aside. The man stumbled and hit the back of the door. His astonished expression was like that of a bird flown into a brick wall.

Fear and anger knotted inside her. If the baron searched the place, he would undoubtedly find his wife. The retribution would be fierce, and Ellie could do nothing to stop it.

She needed to summon more men. Enough to forcibly remove the baron. She scanned the floor just as Baron Willoughby grasped her arm to growl in her ear. "Move aside, bitch. No one keeps me from my wife."

"Remove your hands from the lady."

Ellie turned at the dark, masculine voice. Hugh stood tall and solid, a look of fury clouding his hard features. Relief washed over her, immediate and sure.

"This is not your fight," the baron said.

"I said remove your hand." Hugh's voice resounded with the force of a whip.

Around them, the casino fell eerily silent. Members turned to stare. The crack of the dice ceased, even the roulette wheel stopped spinning. All eyes followed the unfolding scene with keen interest and anticipation.

Baron Willoughby released Ellie's arm, and she stepped back. She suppressed the urge to rub her arm where his cruel fingers had dug into her flesh.

The brute glanced at Ellie, then glared at Hugh. "I'm not interested in her. I want my wife. Now."

"She also said to leave."

Perhaps if the baron were sober, he'd notice the deadly gleam in Hugh's gaze.

They stared each other down, one angry male against another. The contrast was riveting. Hugh was younger, but no less threatening, and for the first time, she could clearly see the military bearing in his stance and in the hard glint in his eyes. The baron was older and used to being a master in his own domain, especially when it came to his fragile wife.

Hugh spoke slowly, as if restraining himself. "I won't repeat myself."

Instead of listening, Baron Willoughby took a step forward and raised his fist. It was a mistake.

Hugh dodged the blow and struck out. A *crack* sounded

as the baron stumbled and fell backward. He clutched his nose, and blood seeped through his fingers. "You bastard! You broke my nose!"

Hugh responded with fire. "You're fortunate that's all I broke. Get out. Now. Do not return and *never* touch the lady again."

Baron Willoughby turned, tripped once, then fled the Raven Club into the street as if a pack of wild hounds were snapping at his heels. Ellie watched wide-eyed, mouth agape.

Hugh turned around and waved to the crowd in a reassuring manner. The club's members returned to their tables and resumed their gambling as if nothing untoward had occurred.

Then he turned to her, all the rage gone from his expression. His gaze passed quickly over her form and returned to her eyes. "God, Ellie. Are you all right?"

"I am. Thank you." She hated that her voice was shaking. She knew he was talented in the ring, but the way he had dispatched the baron was not something she could easily forget.

"Where is his wife?" Hugh asked, his voice gentle.

A lie sprang to her lips, but she knew it was no use. Not after he'd bloodied the baron's nose and tossed him out. Plus, according to Hugh, she had a "tell."

Ellie took a deep breath, then lowered her voice. "She is in the boxing room."

"Come." He took her hand. There was heat and urgency and relief in his touch. She'd taken off her gloves when she'd worked on the ledgers, and she was glad not to have them now. His grasp was comforting, a solid presence beside her. She'd worry about these feelings later, after the shock of the baron's visit had passed, and after they dealt with his wife who was still in the club. He led her to the back of the casino and the boxing room, where they found Lady Willoughby in hysterics.

The woman was pacing the room, clenching her fingers together until her knuckles were pure white. "He knows! He'll find me. I shall not survive this."

Ellie attempted to calm her. "It's all right. Baron Willoughby never saw you, and I denied your presence here tonight. He was deep in his cups."

Lady Willoughby continued to shake her head and weep. A glint of candlelight from the cracked door illuminated her face, and Hugh hissed at the sight of her bruises. "He did this to you?"

Lady Willoughby didn't answer, but fresh tears started anew. "It doesn't matter. None of it matters now."

Hugh reached into his coat, withdrew a handkerchief, and handed it to her. "Here. Let me see. I'm a pugilist. I know bruises." He pulled up a wooden stool and motioned for the lady to sit.

To Ellie's surprise, Lady Willoughby didn't protest but sat on the stool and allowed Hugh to squat before her and study her injuries.

"There, now. Blow your nose. I will not think you unladylike," he said.

Lady Willoughby obliged and wiped her eyes, then loudly blew her nose.

Ellie watched as Hugh calmed the woman and examined her bruises with gentleness. "If it is any consolation, he will have blackened eyes himself tomorrow."

A small smile turned the corners of the lady's lips. "This may sound shocking, but I've often wondered how he would feel if he was the one bloodied and bruised."

Ellie stared, fascinated, as Hugh cared for the lady like a bird with a broken wing. Never had she dreamed he could be this way. This was the Hugh of her youth, only better.

In control, yet caring. Fiercely protective, yet gentle.

Her heart pounded an erratic rhythm.

"Excuse me a moment, my lady." He stood and took Ellie's arm and led her away. She followed him to a corner, far away from where Lady Willoughby sat perched upon the stool.

"You've done this before, haven't you?" Hugh looked down at her, and his green eyes seemed to glow in the dim lighting.

She knew he'd have questions. She'd hidden a beaten wife in the boxing room, then unsuccessfully confronted the woman's furious husband at the door to the Raven Club. Once again, the thought of lying crossed her mind, then fled. Dishonesty seemed wrong now.

"No," she said. "I've never had to deal with an angry, drunken spouse in the past."

He glared at her like he wanted to throttle her. "Not that. You help these women. That's what the hidden room is for, the bed?"

Silence. Her thoughts scampered like leaves in a strong wind, and she struggled with what to say.

"Isn't it?" he demanded.

"Yes," she blurted out.

He hesitated, then his gaze changed to something she was hard-pressed to identify. "I admire you."

Admire? She'd expected many responses from Hugh, but not *that*.

"You seek to give them a few hours of refuge," he said.

She sought to do much more, but she held her tongue. She still couldn't trust him completely. If he knew of their plans—to fake the woman's death and squirrel her away in the country—there was a good chance he would disapprove. She couldn't take the risk. Too much was at stake, including Lady Willoughby's life. She was grateful for his assistance with the baron, but she could not afford to lose focus of her goals. They were too important.

The women were too important.

She needed to lie now, to look him square in the face and suppress the twitch of her lips that he seemed to identify as no one else had.

"Yes," she said. "A few hours of respite. Lady Willoughby never made it that far."

Hugh took Ellie's arm, and together they returned to Lady Willoughby's side. The lady wrung Hugh's handkerchief in her fists. The cotton square would surely be ruined.

"What Lady Ellie has said is true," Hugh said. "The baron was drunk. He is also nursing a broken nose tonight. He will not recall everything that has occurred."

"Then will you take me home?" Lady Willoughby asked, her voice laced with desperation. "Time is of the essence. If the baron finds me in my bedchamber, then he will assume he was wrong and that I was not here tonight."

Ellie didn't want the lady to return home, but she hadn't yet heard from Violet Lasher. Until they had a solid plan to arrange for her escape from London, they had little choice. She looked to Hugh for confirmation, then nodded.

"We will see you safely home," Hugh said.

Minutes later, they were traveling at a swift pace in Hugh's carriage. As soon as they reached Lady Willoughby's Mayfair home, she flew up the front steps and disappeared inside.

"I fear for her," Ellie said.

"Not tonight. The baron will be dealing with his own injuries."

"What about tomorrow? When he is sober, hurting, and dangerously mad?"

"I plan to pay him a visit tomorrow, to have a stern talk, and to ensure he doesn't harm a hair on his wife's head."

She raised her lashes. She understood what he meant

when he said he would speak with the baron. Hugh was going to threaten the man to keep his fists away from his wife. She stared, complete surprise on her face. He was an ever-changing mystery. A man who had sworn to defeat her, then went out of his way to aid a woman in need. A man who'd called her *admirable*. "You would do that?"

"Why do you look so surprised?"

"It's just that...I didn't expect you to be concerned with the welfare of a lady you just met."

"I detest anyone preying on those physically unable to defend themselves."

So did she. Not for the first time, she wondered about his military years and how he had treated the men in his command. Without a doubt, she knew he would have put his men's welfare above his own. The Marquess of Deveril protected the downtrodden.

Hugh hadn't judged her for aiding the baroness but had helped her. She could never have handled the drunken baron, brought his wife home so quickly, and she could never pay a visit and convince the man to leave his wife alone. Maybe they didn't have to arrange for Lady Willoughby's false demise after all.

She leaned forward and placed a hand on Hugh's sleeve. "I'm grateful for your assistance tonight."

"I meant what I said. I admire your efforts, but I don't want you to put yourself in danger."

"It's never happened before."

She felt the muscles in his forearm tense. "But it can occur again. What if I wasn't there tonight? The thought of anything happening to you makes me ill." He held out his hands, and to her shock he was shaking.

The notion of such a big, strong man shaking because he feared for her made her senses spin. She'd seen him fight Bear in the boxing ring. He hadn't shown fear. His fists had been solid and sure.

But now they trembled.

For her.

He fisted his fingers, his callused knuckles stark. Nicks and cuts marred the tanned skin. The hands of a pugilist, not a marquess.

"Ellie," he said simply.

She reached out and took his hands. They were double the size of hers. She ran her thumb back and forth across his bruised knuckles. He hissed in a breath and wove his fingers through hers.

"You asked me if I thought of our kiss, and I told you I hadn't. I lied," she whispered.

He was still beside her. Only his green eyes were intense and fierce. "How much have you thought of it?"

"A lot."

The green irises darkened, drawing her in. "Good. Because I want to kiss you again. May I?"

She swallowed, her nervousness rising, but something else sizzled just beneath the surface, something impossible to deny. A clawing need that had nothing to do with their competition, but a base desire deep inside her. Perhaps it was the near rescue, the need that arose when he'd stepped in to help her tonight, or even more tormenting, his plan to visit the baron tomorrow to ensure another's safety. Whatever the reasons, she did not want to deny the most basic contact between them.

"Yes," she whispered. "I'd like that."

Chapter Nine

Ellie tugged on their entwined fingers and leaned toward him until their faces were only inches apart. Her heart pounded. She knew any type of intimacy with Hugh was wrong, very wrong, but she pushed her worries aside. Tonight was different. He was different.

He'd called her *admirable.*

The air rushed from her lungs as he met her halfway until their faces were only inches apart. The scent of his cologne and soap and something else...something she thought was dangerous male, teased her senses. Desire illuminated his forest-green eyes. Her gaze dropped to his mouth, the sensual curve of his full lips, and the tantalizing divot in his chin. She had an irresistible urge to lick the masculine mark.

A lock of dark hair rested on his forehead and gave him a roguish appearance. Without thought, she reached out and smoothed it in place.

He let out a breath. "Careful, Ellie. I might take you at your word about that kiss."

She tilted her head to the side and studied him. "You

asked and I said yes."

She took a breath of confidence, then before she lost her nerve, leaned even closer until only a wisp of air separated them. He held still as if he expected her to pull back and flee like a madwoman from the carriage at any moment. Perhaps she was mad. This insane urge to kiss him grew stronger with every passing second.

Instead of resisting, her eyes fluttered and she met his lips, desperate for the taste of him. He was gentle at first, his lips firm but closed. It wasn't enough. Thoughts of their shared kiss had invaded her dreams, and she wanted more.

Her tongue darted out to outline his lips. He expelled a breath, and his hand reached up to pull her head closer as he opened his mouth to her tongue. She delved inside to explore his mouth and was rewarded when he met her tongue with his. Her hands slid up his arms around his shoulders, her fingers finding the muscles in the nape of his neck and his dark hair. She tilted her head to the side, eager for more.

He groaned and pulled her onto his lap. Even through the layers of her gown and his trousers, she was aware of his heat. And his hardness. It should frighten her, make her shove him away. Instead, she was lost, adrift in a sea of emotion. She struggled to find purchase, to keep a deep part of her hidden and sheltered from the overpowering male pressed against her. With every stroke of his tongue, he battered against her defenses.

No. She couldn't travel down that path of heartache again. She wasn't that foolish, was she?

But he had learned of her plans, and he hadn't lectured or berated her, or heaven forbid, run straight to Ian. He'd aided her when she'd needed it most.

And his kisses felt heavenly. His lips traveled a path down to her ear and he suckled her sensitive lobe. Her knees felt weak. If she weren't already sprawled across his lap, she would have fallen. A rush of heat flooded between her legs. His mouth continued its torturous path to her neck, down to the swell of her breasts above her bodice. Her nipples tightened beneath the fabric. He kissed her there, his mouth hovering above the satin.

She wished there was no silk between them. If his kisses were wonderful on her lips, her nape, the skin above her bodice, then what would they feel like on her naked breast?

She wanted his mouth there, wanted his lips to caress her aching flesh.

"Your skin is so soft." He caressed her cheek.

"And here." His hands moved to her throat.

"And most definitely here." He slipped a finger inside her bodice and stroked her nipple. She was gasping for more.

"God, how I want you. I've wanted you forever."

Truly? She knew better than to trust the seductively dangerous words from his mouth.

"But I'll not take you in a carriage. We're back at the club, love."

She didn't know what was more shocking. That they had arrived or that he called her *love*.

Her eyes widened, and she slipped off his lap and back onto her bench. She smoothed her skirts, her hair, then dared to look at him.

His mouth curved in an arrogantly male smile. "Are you going to deny liking that kiss?"

"A true gentleman would not ask."

"After tonight, I believe we are beyond propriety."

"Because of what just occurred in this carriage? I don't believe—"

"No. Because of what occurred in the club. The next time you plan to shield a beaten woman, I want to know about it."

"I hardly think your request is—"

"I wasn't asking."

She blinked in surprise. Gone was the gentle but consuming lover. The man who'd whispered huskily into her ear that he'd wanted her. His voice was hard as steel as he looked at her. His expression was that of an officer, a man in charge.

"I cannot promise you that."

"You are beyond promising. Baron Willoughby is dangerous. You don't know what you are getting into."

"And you have my interests in mind?"

"Yes."

She glared at him.

"Don't cross me in this." Then he pressed his lips to hers. Like flint striking steel, a fiery need licked at her. He pulled back, and the hunger in his gaze was unmistakable. Raw and primitive.

Her weak body cried out for more.

She was accustomed to shielding her heart, her soul. She'd had five years of practice since finding Hugh kissing another in the gardens of a ball. She'd feared having her heart crushed again by the broken promises of a selfish rogue.

But this time was different.

This time, she was afraid of herself.

• • •

"I heard there was trouble at the club last night," Grace said.

Ellie stood by her sister-in-law's bedside. She'd come to visit and had brought a steaming cup of chocolate. She knew Grace preferred chocolate over coffee, and she'd hoped the drink and the company would cheer her.

Grace had been bedridden for four days. She was an energetic person by nature and enjoyed walks and working on the club's numerous ledgers in Ian's upstairs office. She hadn't been able to do much but rest and read since she'd experienced pain in her lower back. The family physician, as well as Ian, had been concerned.

Yet somehow, Grace had learned of the problem at the club last night.

"Brooks told you," Ellie said.

Grace looked her up and down and pushed a lock of dark hair from her face. She eased back on the mound of pillows supporting her in a sitting position, her legs crossing on the bed. "No. Brooks wasn't there, and you know it."

"Then how?"

"Simon sent word."

"Who?" As soon as the question was out of Ellie's mouth, she knew the answer. Simon was the liveried guard at the door who had taken Brooks's place. The man Baron Willoughby had tossed aside like a sack of grain.

Grace continued to watch, a keen glimmer in her eye. "The Marquess of Deveril took care of Lord Willoughby."

Ellie took a deep breath. "Yes, he did."

Grace's hands ran over her distended stomach in a circular motion, the movement smooth and comforting. "Perhaps you should give the marquess a second chance, Ellie."

"No," she blurted out without hesitation. A kiss was not a sufficient reason to expose herself to heartache again. She was a mature woman who could make her own decisions, and sharing a heated moment during a carriage ride—no matter how wondrous—was not sufficient reason to alter the course of her life. She knew what she longed for, and financial independence was not something she was willing to sacrifice.

"People change. It was years ago." Grace's hands ceased moving to rest at her sides. "I saw the way he looked at you."

"What way?"

"The way Ian looked at me the first time. Like a man who knows what he wants. I didn't understand it then, but now I do."

Her words burned, branding themselves into her mind. "No. You're wrong. The Marquess of Deveril only wants one thing: the Raven Club."

"Hmm. He came to your aid last evening, didn't he?"

"Just because he used his brute strength to toss out a foolish, drunken lord does not mean he has changed his ways."

"Asinine lord."

"Pardon?"

Grace waved a hand. "Baron Willoughby is asinine. I never liked him."

"Well, that makes two of us then." Ellie disliked Baron Willoughby immensely, and she wondered if Grace knew how the man treated his young wife. She dismissed the thought. Samantha Willoughby hid her bruises well, and she would never speak of her troubles to others.

Ellie was more convinced than before that she had to keep her plans to help Lady Willoughby secret. Grace was more accepting than Ellie's brother, but if either learned of her association with Violet Lasher, all would be lost.

Ian would go berserk.

"How are your endeavors at the Raven Club?" Grace asked, changing the subject.

Ellie plumped the pillows behind Grace, grateful to have a task while her mind churned with how best to handle the topic of discussion. "My plans are coming along. I do believe Ian will have no choice but to find my efforts are most profitable."

"Hmm. We will both have a say."

Ellie handed Grace the cup of chocolate. "You'll pick me, won't you, Grace?" She hoped she didn't sound as desperate as she felt. She schooled her expression and tried to look as she must. Confident, competent, and determined to win.

Grace sipped the hot drink. "I must be fair."

"Of course." She felt a stab of disappointment. Ellie knew her plans for the club would work. They must. But deep down, she'd always hoped Grace would champion her.

Had she been wrong?

Rather than encourage her, Grace had suggested she give Hugh a second chance. Their encounter in the carriage returned in a flash. All during the night, she'd relived the heady sensation of his lips pressed against hers, tender and light as a summer breeze. And when their embrace had heated and he'd captured her lips with demanding mastery, she'd returned his kiss with reckless abandon. She had told him she wanted to kiss him, and she had no regrets at the time.

Her regrets came soon afterward, when he'd changed from a charming and seductive man to an arrogant and highhanded marquess. His demeanor had taken her off guard, and she'd felt pushed into a corner. He'd demanded that she tell him the next time a woman in danger came to her at the Raven Club.

Not bloody likely.

Grace continued to take small sips of her chocolate, watching Ellie over the rim of her cup. Ellie grew nervous, as if her sister-in-law could read her thoughts. She reached for the tray on the end table, intending to remove it, when she spotted a book. She picked it up and gave Grace a skeptical look. "Shakespeare's *Romeo and Juliet*?"

"Ian is reading it to me."

"Good heavens, why? It's a tragedy." Couldn't her brother find something more uplifting to read to his expectant wife? Something with a happy ending?

Grace lowered her cup and sighed dreamily. "Two young lovers are very romantic."

"But they both die!"

"So? They die in love."

The pregnancy must be doing something to her mind. Ellie also thought the entire story foolish. Men were inherently selfish. What man would stab himself to death over the loss of a lover? She had loved Hugh, she'd thought he loved her as well, but then he crushed her hopes and dreams in one night and walked away from her without a backward glance.

Ellie set the book down. "I'm worried about you."

Grace angled her head. "Don't be. Women have been giving birth from the beginning of time."

And many have died from it.

Ellie bit her tongue. "Still, the family physician insists you stay in bed. Why?"

For the first time, concern marred Grace's brow. "It wasn't the physician. Mrs. Henderson recommended bed rest."

"Who?"

"Mrs. Henderson is my midwife. I trust her more than any male physician. She said the babe has not turned and can make for a difficult birth."

"Oh, Grace." Ellie felt the color drain from her face. Fear flooded her like a strong storm.

"It's early still. We cannot say what will happen until it is time."

"And if not?"

"Then I will be in Mrs. Henderson's capable hands," Grace said. "I'm telling you this because I need you to do two things for me. First, I need you to keep Ian calm during the birth."

Ellie's eyebrows shot upward. "Keep him calm! Do you not know my brother?"

Ian was madly in love with his wife. If he had any idea…

Ellie swallowed. Grace was bedridden. The least Ellie could do was assure her sister-in-law not to worry over her husband. "I shall do all I can. I will also ensure Brooks keeps my brother in the drawing room smoking cigars and drinking whisky when your time comes."

"Good. I do not wish for Ian to scowl at Mrs. Henderson and chase her away. I know how intimidating my husband can be."

"What is your second request?"

Something flickered in Grace's eyes, something distant and disturbing. "If something should happen to me during the birth"—Grace held up a hand when Ellie was about to protest—"and I don't believe it will, but if it does, I need you to look after Ian."

"Don't speak like that." Her fear increased tenfold. The fact that Grace would even bring up such a horrific ending to her pregnancy made her stomach sink.

"Nonsense. We are women, and we are stronger than men. You are the most responsible. Olivia is fanciful, far too adventurous, and young." Grace clutched Ellie's hand. "Promise."

"I can't!"

Grace squeezed her fingers, the tightness almost painful. "Yes, you can. Ian has already experienced a lifetime of guilt and worry over Matthew's death. There's no need for him to feel guilty over me as well."

Matthew. Their oldest brother—the brother who was supposed to inherit the earldom. He'd had a fondness for racing horses and had fallen off his horse, struck his head, and died. Ellie knew of the rumors: that Ian had lured Matthew to the treacherous track known as Devil's Leap in order to murder his brother and seize the title.

Lies. All vicious lies.

No one had loved Matthew more than Ian. For some reason their father, the old earl, had hated Ian, but the brothers' bond had remained strong. Ian had left home to open the Raven Club, and Matthew had been groomed for the earldom.

"The gossips are nothing but harpies. Ian would never have harmed Matthew. He tried to save him." Ellie's voice was hoarse.

"I know. But you need to look after Ian."

Ellie nodded. "I promise."

Grace exhaled a shuddering breath. "Good. Meanwhile, Lady Emberly's garden party is tomorrow. You are attending with Olivia, correct?"

"Yes." Lady Emberly was a close family friend. She was also one of the few society hostesses who had supported Ian as the Earl of Castleton after Matthew's death.

"You should know that I also sent word to the dowager," Grace said.

Ellie blinked. "My mother? She is in Bath with my aunt."

"She will want to see her grandchild."

She would. The dowager would be thrilled at the birth of her first grandchild. Ellie's thoughts suddenly turned. Her mother would also be furious if she learned Ellie was in a contest with the Marquess of Deveril to win the Raven Club. Her mother had wanted Ellie to wed years ago. She'd also wanted Ian to sell the Raven Club before he married Grace.

Thankfully, that had never occurred.

Ellie stood. "I shall return tomorrow with another book."

Grace lowered her cup, angling her face at Ellie. "Good luck at the Raven, Ellie. I wish I could be there to watch you work."

"You taught me all I know about the ledgers. I'll forever be grateful." Ellie kissed Grace on the cheek and rested a hand on her stomach. Her eyes widened as she felt a flutter of movement beneath her palm. "My niece or nephew is quite active."

Grace's lips curved. "Ian wants a girl, but I think it's a boy."

For a stabbing instant, trepidation returned and queasiness churned her stomach. She feared for Grace. And Ian.

Sweet lord, Ian couldn't lose Grace. He would be devastated. His guilt would be overwhelming. Nothing Ellie could do would be able to help him. Her brother would be tossed into an ocean of despair so deep, she didn't think he'd return. It would be worse than when Matthew died. Much worse. Grace was his soul mate, the love of his life, the woman who saved him from a life of loneliness and reckless behavior. Ian had only known the Raven Club and believed the casino was all he'd needed in life. Until Grace had walked into his office and insisted on paying off her father's debts and demanding Ian refuse her sire membership and a seat at the tables.

Ellie forced a smile. No sense letting Grace see her fears.

All would be well.

It had to be. The alternative was unthinkable. God couldn't be that cruel, could he?

Ellie picked up the empty tray and turned to leave.

"One more thing," Grace called out.

Ellie hesitated, her hand grazing the door handle. "Yes?"

"Keep in mind what I said about the marquess. From what I discerned, he wants more than just to win the club."

Chapter Ten

The tinkle of laughter grated on Ellie's nerves. She sipped a glass of overly sweet lemonade and scanned Lady Emberly's vast lawns. The garden party was to celebrate the hostess's new glass-and-steel garden conservatory, which housed her prized rosebushes. It was a lovely day, as if their hostess had commanded the weather herself. The sun shone brightly, and not a cloud marred the lovely blue sky.

Ellie had never been more miserable. Her conversation with Grace, combined with the recurring memories of Hugh's kiss, had made her uneasy. It had been three long days, so why couldn't she forget his kiss?

She felt the beginnings of a headache, and she rubbed her right temple.

Ladies and gentlemen strolled the gardens. Tables had been carried outside by servants, and all types of delicacies that had been prepared by Lady Emberly's French chef were on display—a variety of meats and poultry, seasoned asparagus and tender French beans, fish in delicate lemon and caper sauce, and pastries.

She'd attended out of obligation, not pleasure. Ellie smoothed her skirts with hopes that the motion would comfort her. She'd settled for a silk dress with a ruffled hem, dyed a rich blue. The heart-shaped bodice was artfully cut to reveal the swell of her breasts. Yet her stays felt tied too tightly, and each breath was a struggle in the warm, humid air.

Perhaps she needed food. She'd only nibbled on a piece of toast this morning and had washed it down with a cup of weak tea. If she ate, she believed her headache would subside and she could enjoy the party. Maybe she could even join Lady Emberly's tour of the conservatory to observe her rosebushes.

Ellie set her empty glass on a passing tray of a liveried footman, then headed toward the laden table. She was halfway across the lawn when she noticed Olivia waving. A shaft of sunlight highlighted a gleam of her sister's fair hair, casting her in an ethereal glow. Ellie sighed, torn between sustenance and her sister.

Olivia's summons won.

Ellie approached. "Is all well?"

Olivia grasped her arm and tugged her behind a potted tree, then scanned the area to be sure they would not be overheard.

"Olivia!"

Satisfied they were alone, Olivia met her eyes. "I don't know what you did, but Lady Willoughby is more at ease."

"I did not do anything."

She didn't. Hugh had. He'd said he would speak to Baron Willoughby. He must have made good on his promise. She ignored the telltale tightening of her throat at the thought of him helping them that night and following through with his intentions to visit the baron.

"Is Lady Willoughby here?" Ellie hadn't seen her, but she

hadn't walked the entire perimeter of the gardens yet.

"No. She declined the invitation."

"Wait. When you say Lady Willoughby is at ease, do you mean she is happy?"

Olivia looked at her, her green eyes trained on her face. "Happy? No. But more relaxed. Samantha doesn't jump at the slightest sound or the scruff of boots on the floor. Her bruises are fading as well."

"Thank the lord for that much."

"It started after she attended the Raven Club. What happened?" Olivia asked.

Ellie's mind turned back to that night. "The Marquess of Deveril tossed an intoxicated Baron Willoughby out of the club. Deveril also said he would speak with the baron about the treatment of his wife. It must have been a strong, one-sided discussion."

"Whatever he did, it worked. The baron hasn't come near her, let alone raised a fist to her."

"Good." A tittering of a group of young women drew Ellie's attention. "Is it time for Lady Emberly's conservatory tour?"

"Not quite."

Ellie looked over her sister's shoulder, then froze at the sight of the Marquess of Deveril himself just inside the garden gate. Dressed in a blue coat with a striped waistcoat, trousers, and snowy cravat, he was striking. He carried himself with confidence, and even in a crowd, his appearance was compelling. His dark hair had an unruly wave that only added to his rugged good looks. He took a step forward and greeted Lady Emberly.

"What is he doing here?" Ellie's voice sounded hoarse to her own ears.

Olivia shrugged. "He's made a few social events since his return from the army. Perhaps his family had been acquainted with Lady Emberly."

From the excited look of the females present, she was not the only one to notice his appearance. The older matrons called their daughters, and they eagerly fluttered to their mothers' sides. The widows gave him sly looks. Some approached, and he bowed and smiled.

A sourness settled in the pit of her stomach as Ellie watched the ladies respond to his charm. "They're making fools of themselves," she said, her voice hoarse.

Olivia rubbed her chin. "Do you blame them? He is a marquess and a most eligible bachelor."

A group of women had wandered closer to where they stood. No doubt to get a better look at Hugh.

"Deveril is quite handsome," a tall brunette said as she fanned herself.

"His last mistress was an actress."

"No. It was a dressmaker to the actress," a fair-haired woman countered.

"Perhaps it was both."

High-pitched tittering sounded behind fluttering fans. It put Ellie's nerves on end.

"He must wed someday," the fair-haired woman said wistfully.

"You already have a husband," the brunette pointed out.

"He's hard of hearing."

"At least he's hard somewhere. Unlike mine," a third woman said.

More coarse laughter.

Something about the third woman's lilting voice caught Ellie's attention. The hair on her nape stood on end, as if in warning.

It can't be.

Ellie shifted to see Isabelle, Lady Fabry, standing with the group of ladies.

Ellie's throat seemed to close up, and her breasts rose and fell as her breath became labored. The years hadn't changed Isabelle's looks. She remained a vivid brunette with a voluptuous figure. She'd married a man thirty years her senior who was hard of hearing and carried a thick quizzing glass that dangled from his waistcoat. From what Ellie had heard, the woman hadn't changed much in personality, either. Fortunately, Isabelle hadn't noticed her. She was too busy mocking her elderly husband and staring at Hugh.

Ellie had attended previous society functions where Isabelle had also been in attendance, but Ellie had been careful to avoid her. This time was different. This was the first time that Hugh was present.

Isabelle left her friends and headed straight for Hugh. Ellie watched, and the world seemed to fade, seemed to recede in her mind as if the years melted away and she was observing a scene from her past unfold right before her. A scene she'd desperately tried to forget and failed to over the course of five long years.

Isabelle glided forward and halted before the Marquess of Deveril. Her painted lips curled in a coy smile, and she curtsied, her breasts nearly spilling from her scandalously low-cut bodice. He bowed and greeted her.

Ellie turned away, unwilling to watch, unwilling to have the tiny tears in her heart rip open further. Her headache slid to the base of her skull, increased in intensity, and began to pound in a rhythm that matched her heart. "I don't feel well," she blurted out. "I believe a walk in the gardens is what I need."

Olivia looked at her with pity, her brow creasing in concern. "Shall I accompany you?"

Her sister must have seen, must know, but Ellie didn't want to speak of it. The urge to flee was too powerful. Shame for her reaction at the mere the sight of the pair together was enough to make her want to run and hide. Her sister's pity was almost as unbearable.

Had she not learned anything?

"No. Please. Solitude is what I require," she choked out.

So far, Hugh hadn't seen her. If she was fortunate, she could slip into the gardens, find a stone bench, and rest until he grew bored, or an hour passed and he left the garden party.

Or until Isabelle insisted upon his escort during the conservatory tour. Her elderly husband wouldn't even notice her absence and was probably inside Lady Emberly's home napping in the drawing room.

She slipped away to follow a path into the meticulously manicured gardens. It was cooler here, beneath the canopy of towering trees, and Ellie let out a held-in breath. Soon the sound of running water drew her, and she strolled toward a fountain and a pond filled with tiny, colorful fish. Several minutes passed as she watched exotic blue, yellow, and orange fish dart beneath the smooth rocks that lined the bottom of a man-made pond. She spotted a stone bench sheltered by an ancient oak and sat. A cool breeze tickled tendrils of hair that had escaped her nape. Several minutes passed as she watched the fish and pushed thoughts of Hugh and Isabelle from her mind. Her headache was still present but had subsided to a distant ache.

"I've been looking for you."

She froze at the sound of the familiar masculine voice.

Hugh appeared from around a tree to stand by her bench. Her heart squeezed at the sight of him—dark hair, chiseled features, wide, sensual mouth, and captivating green eyes. It took every ounce of willpower not to jump to her feet and seek the sanctuary of the gardens. She wouldn't act the coward.

"I sought solitude."

"Ah, I didn't mean to disturb you, but I saw you flee."

She stood to face him, chin held high. "I didn't run away."

He cocked an eyebrow in an arrogant manner that infuriated her. "Good. Because I feared you spotted me and ran."

She laughed, a high-pitched sound. "Never. Why are you here?"

"We should talk about what happened in the carriage."

"We said all that needs to be said about the matter. The next time I plan to shield a beaten woman, you want to be informed."

"You did not promise, as I recall."

"You recall correctly."

"Stubborn as ever."

He shot her an all-too-familiar devilish grin. She should despise him for the ease and smoothness for which his lips curved. He was a man confident with the fair sex. She had no doubt he'd known more than his share—in and out of the bedroom.

Isabelle immediately came to mind.

Hugh broke the silence, his sharp eyes watching her. "I want you to know that you are the only woman on my mind."

Her stomach tightened. Why would he say such a thing?

Unless he knew she spotted him with Isabelle, knew how much the mere sight of the woman disturbed her. No matter how many years had passed, Ellie's gut still tightened in anticipation of a painful blow. And to see Hugh speak with her? Ellie would rather die a thousand deaths than see the two of them in the same room together. She needn't subject herself to such misery.

"I attended Lady Emberly's party because I knew you would be here," he said. "I stopped by your brother's residence, and he mentioned you and your sister had accepted an invitation. I headed here straightaway."

"Why?"

"We should speak about our kiss. It's been on my mind."

Was he serious? Or was he manipulating her? Was everything a game of conquest for the Marquess of Deveril?

"It's of little consequence. Not worth discussing or thinking about."

Liar. She'd thought of little else.

"Hmm," he said simply, as if he knew her thoughts. His gaze roamed an unhurried path over her features. She could feel the heat graze her cheek, then her lips, and her pulse quickened. "I think you're lying."

"You do not know me."

He chuckled, a deep sound that vibrated through her body. "To the contrary, I think I do know you. Shall I demonstrate how well?"

"What does that mean?"

Rather than kiss her, he raised her hand to his lips and pressed a kiss to her gloved hand. Even through the satin, her skin prickled pleasurably and her breathing grew shallow. A slow burn began in her stomach then spread to her limbs and the secret place between her legs. She felt her face heat. She hated that her body reacted this way to him. And he must know, damn him.

"It's only about you, Ellie."

Her heart pounded in her chest so forcefully she wondered if he could hear. It was as if he knew her deepest insecurities and was spewing what she needed to hear.

He knew.

He'd seen her flee. He knew how much the mere presence of Isabelle disturbed her. He knew, and he was trying to ease her torment.

"Do you believe me?"

Did she? Looking into his eyes, he seemed sincere, but she also knew she wasn't the best judge of men. How could she be when he'd been the one to show her just how foolish she could be?

And what of the Raven Club? Nothing changed the fact that they were rivals. A fateful night in which they both helped a battered woman in need, a kiss in a carriage on the way home—neither event changed her goals.

"It no longer matters." And with that final statement, she turned on her heel and fled the gardens.

Chapter Eleven

Hugh walked into a tavern and chose an empty table in the corner. The tavern was doing a brisk business tonight, and several tables were crowded with men wearing corduroy jackets and patched trousers who had arrived straight from the factories to drink their ale. Well-dressed young gentlemen sat at another table, deep in their cups, exchanging crude jokes and coarse laughter. University fops away from school.

Hugh was in no mood for company. His thoughts were consumed with the Raven Club, but not with his plans for the boxing room.

With Ellie.

He'd told her the truth that afternoon. He had attended Lady Emberly's garden party because he knew Ellie would be there. He needed to speak with her, and he wanted to do it away from the club, away from the place where her competitive nature flourished and was a constant reminder of both of their goals.

Things were changing between them, at least for him. The night he'd discovered her hidden activities to protect Lady

Willoughby had opened his eyes. He began to understand more of why she desperately wanted to win the club. She'd put herself in danger to aid another for a few hours of respite in her hidden room. He hadn't lied when he'd called her admirable. But that didn't mean he'd approve of her putting herself at risk. His mind had clouded at the thought, and he'd wanted to pull her into his arms and kiss sense into her.

Thank God she'd consented. But what had started as a simple kiss had quickly changed. Her kisses had affected him even more than he thought they would. She was brave, loyal, and oh so stubborn.

Most men would find the last trait undesirable in a woman. They sought compliance, complicity, a stable household.

Not Hugh. He would find a docile partner boring and not one who would hold his interest for long.

No matter how admirable, he could never condone Ellie's dangerous activities. Hiding a lady, even for the evening, was risky. Baron Willoughby had been angry, jealous, and drunk—a volatile combination in any man, let alone a bastard like him. A man that treated his wife the way the baron had hurt his wasn't worth the dirt beneath Hugh's boot. And when he'd glared at Ellie with fury, Hugh wanted to tear the man from limb to limb.

A buxom, blond tavern maid approached with a tray of ale. "A drink, me lord?"

He nodded and she leaned far over the table as she placed the mug before her, her ample breasts on display in her low bodice. "Anything else I can get ye, me lord?"

Not long ago, he would have been tempted. He would have easily accepted her offer and eased his worries in a warm, willing body. But now he found himself unmoved by her…unmoved by the thought of any other woman.

"Just the ale."

She looked at him, her bold stare trained on his face.

"Ah, a lady has seized your heart."

"Hardly," Hugh scoffed. "I've business on my mind."

She gave him a sly look that said she didn't believe a word out of his mouth. She took her leave, her hips sashaying toward the kitchens. He wanted to call her back and argue.

Just because he did not want to see Ellie hurt, did not mean she'd seized his heart.

Damn.

His mind turned as he drank from the tankard. It wasn't just Baron Willoughby that bothered him. Things hadn't gone as he'd planned at the garden party, either, and soon after he'd stepped foot through the garden gate, he'd been waylaid by Lady Fabry. He'd seen the moment Ellie had spotted Isabelle beside him. Ellie's delicate brow had furrowed, her eyes had widened with astonishment, not with joy or recognition, but with torment, and she'd fled into the gardens.

Without a thought, he'd followed her.

He'd wanted to tell her Lady Fabry meant nothing to him—then or now. But how? And would she believe him?

Instinct told him never to bring up Isabelle or speak her name, but to somehow confirm that Ellie was the only woman on his mind.

She hadn't believed him. Or at least, she hadn't wanted to. In her mind, she'd returned to a place from years ago, a different hostess's garden, and the event that had altered both of their futures. He never liked Isabelle and he hadn't enjoyed their kiss. He'd already told Ellie once, but he knew telling her again without revealing the entire truth would be fruitless and even more harmful.

He hadn't lied today. He could not care less about Isabelle, or any other woman in society.

After returning into Ellie's life, how could it be any other way?

. . .

He was avoiding her.

No matter how hard she tried, she couldn't forget their brief encounter by Lady Emberly's pond. His words had left a mark on her mind just as his kiss had left a tingling on the back of her hand. This attraction to him was perilous and would do her no good. She needed to keep her mind on her goal: the Raven Club. Too much was at stake to behave recklessly and risk heartache.

So she'd kept to herself, careful not to run into Hugh on the casino floor. She'd been successful. At first, she'd thought it was because of her evasive efforts. She'd carefully look out the window onto the casino floor before leaving the second-floor office. If Hugh was within sight, she would remain upstairs. That's when she'd spotted one of the boys who worked in the boxing room open the door to glance out and then return inside. Only then did Hugh step outside.

She felt deflated, a deep, unaccustomed ache in her chest. How could she avoid him, then feel hurt when she discovered he was doing the same?

Her tumultuous thoughts raced. Did he regret what he'd told her in the gardens? Perhaps she wasn't the only woman on his mind? Ellie had claimed a headache and had left the Lady Emberly's home soon after. Had Hugh remained to flirt with his many female admirers, or heaven help her, Lady Fabry?

Ugh.

At least the women's gambling room was near complete. The room had been painted an inviting pale gold, and the gambling tables had arrived. Faro, hazard, and whist tables were now arranged alongside the roulette table. She'd selected croupiers and staff and picked out different liveried uniforms for them to wear to set them apart from the workers in the main casino. A blue dress with silver trim for the female servants and a blue coat and striped waistcoat for the male servants to match the blue silk curtains. Despite what she'd told Hugh, they weren't all men.

It had been a week since the harrowing incident with Baron Willoughby. She hadn't heard a word from Violet Lasher, but for the first time, Ellie wasn't worried. Olivia had visited Lady Willoughby twice and had reported that the baron had kept his distance from his wife.

Perhaps one good thing had resulted from the Marquess of Deveril coming back into her life.

A low knock on the office door drew her attention. "Yes?"

The door opened and Brooks stepped inside, his large frame blocking the doorway. He held a letter in his hand. "This just arrived for you, my lady."

"Thank you."

He hesitated after handing the letter to her, shifting from foot to foot in apparent unease, and she looked up. "Is there something else?"

His square jaw tightened, and darkness clouded his eyes. "I never told you, but I'm sorry I was not here the other night."

She didn't ask. She knew which evening he was referring to. No doubt, if Brooks were guarding the door of the Raven Club a week ago, he could have easily handled the unruly baron. "It was your evening to yourself. You could not have known that Baron Willoughby would appear in such a state."

"Still. I'm glad Deveril was here in my stead."

Must everyone champion Hugh? First Grace, now Brooks. Ellie tried to disguise her annoyance and cleared her throat. She needed to look at things from Brooks's point of view. He was right, of course. Deveril had taken care of matters that evening and had handled the unruly, intoxicated baron. But must Hugh continue to win over those closest to her? Was Olivia next?

She waited until Brooks closed the door behind him and she was alone before opening the letter. The flowery script was unique and recognizable. Violet Lasher had finally written.

Our plans have changed. Meet this afternoon at the tobacconists, Fribourg & Treyer's.

Ellie pinched the foolscap between her thumb and forefinger. What could have changed? Was another lady in need of assistance?

It was possible. Violet's position ensured she had secret knowledge of the aristocracy that Ellie could never dream of obtaining.

Ellie folded the letter and slipped it into her dress pocket. They had never met in such a public place. It must be important for Violet to pick such a location. Moments later, Ellie left the club, walked to the end of the street, and hailed a hackney.

Fribourg & Treyer's tobacconists was located in a busy section of Piccadilly. Men and women strode down the street and in and out of neighboring shops. Ellie couldn't fathom why Violet had picked this location at this time of day. Surely, they would be seen. Even if Violet appeared in her carriage with the shades drawn, there was risk.

The courtesan's news must be urgent. Had something happened to Samantha Willoughby? Or was there another woman in dire need? Feeling a sickening sense of dread to come, Ellie approached the tobacconist shop. The little bell above the door chimed as she opened and closed the door to a gust of wind and stepped inside. A shopkeeper was assisting a middle-aged couple as the man perused a table of snuff.

Ellie feigned interest in the wares displayed on a table across the room where dozens of varieties and flavors of snuff were displayed. She overheard the shopkeeper talking about the different types of snuff—from texture to color to scent. She opened several tins, and the pleasant fragrances of honey, vanilla, apricot, cinnamon, and Attar of Roses teased her senses.

Ian had an intricate gold snuffbox with a hidden compartment that displayed a miniature portrait of Grace. He rarely used snuff, but she knew he occasionally indulged. She randomly selected one tin of snuff scented with orange and decided to gift it to him.

Once again, the shop's bells chimed, and Violet Lasher walked inside. Dressed in a blue dress that enhanced the vivid blue of her eyes, she was striking. Her blond hair was upswept into a mass of curls that appeared somewhat haphazard but artfully arranged at the same time. Her breasts swelled from her tight bodice. All eyes turned to her—the clerk's and his customers'. The husband gaped, and his wife scowled, then slapped him on his arm.

How on earth was Ellie to speak with the courtesan unnoticed?

But Violet was as shrewd as she was stunning. She approached Ellie's table and randomly picked up a tin of snuff without ever making eye contact with her. If anyone looked, it appeared as if they did not know each other.

"Baron Willoughby found his wife's mask," Violet said as she sniffed a tin of camphor-scented snuff.

Ellie froze, then lowered her voice to a mere whisper. "The mask she wore to the Raven Club?"

"Yes. He knows she was there. She does not have much time."

A stab of fear centered in Ellie's chest, and she closed her eyes. When she opened them, Violet was still watching her.

"Good God. What do we do?"

The thought of telling Hugh crossed her mind. He had frightened the baron into staying away from his wife, but this was different. Baron Willoughby knew his wife had lied. He could drink too much and lose his temper at any time. One swing of his fist could end his young wife's life. Even Hugh could not prevent such a tragedy.

"She has to leave London," Violet said.

Ellie steeled herself for Violet's instructions. "How do you intend to fake her death?"

"There is no time. She must go," Violet said.

"Will she agree?"

Violet set down the tin and picked up another. "I believe she is wise enough to recognize her plight."

"When?"

"Two evenings from tonight," Violet said. "She must arrive at the club and you will usher her out the back. My carriage will be waiting for her in the mews."

Two evenings.

That's when Ellie had planned to open her ladies' gambling club. All her hard work and preparation had been in anticipation for that night. Could she do both? Open her room and arrange to ferry Samantha Willoughby to safety? She would have to. Another thought occurred to her: it would be the perfect distraction. No one would notice her missing for an hour. She'd arranged for a competent staff who were well experienced, and Brooks could oversee everything while she claimed she needed to work upstairs.

"It'll work," Ellie said.

Violet waved at the shopkeeper and smiled. The older man left the couple he'd been helping and nearly tripped over his feet in his haste to assist her.

After Violet paid for her purchase and departed, Ellie remained by the table. Her eyes glazed over the tins of snuff.

Her mind was in tumult over what she'd just learned. The shop's bells jingled, but Ellie didn't turn to see who had entered. She had much work to do in two days' time. As if in a daze, she turned to head for the counter to make her purchase, when a hand settled on her elbow.

"I didn't know you preferred snuff."

She whirled to find Hugh standing behind her. Dressed in a brown greatcoat that emphasized his broad shoulders, he watched her. His heated gaze made her breath catch and her belly tighten.

Her eyes narrowed. "Are you following me?"

Chapter Twelve

Hugh's mouth curved in a grin that made Ellie's heart skip a beat. "I should lie and say yes, but the truth is no. My appearance here is a coincidence."

"Hmm."

He eyed the tin in her hand. "You're buying snuff?"

"It is for my brother," she blurted out. Heaven forbid he learn the true reason she was in the tobacconist's shop today. She prayed he hadn't seen Violet Lasher leave.

"The earl prefers Havana snuff."

"Pardon?"

"If you are purchasing it for your brother, the earl will not enjoy orange-scented snuff. He used a pinch of Havana snuff when I first met with him, the same day he told me the Raven Club was for sale."

Her cheeks grew warm. If he was trying to intimidate her, she refused to rise to the bait and give him the satisfaction of a scathing response in public. "Good to know, however, I will keep my selection."

"Of course you will. I would not expect anything else."

"What does that mean?" she asked.

"Only that you are the most stubborn female I have ever met."

She glared at him. "And you are the most infuriating male I've ever known."

"Touché. Come. Let us make our purchases. Then I will see you home."

"You insult me, then decide to act the gentleman?"

Hugh plucked the tin from her hands, then walked toward the counter and the waiting clerk. Moments later, he returned to her side, a package wrapped in brown paper under his arm. "Where is your maid?"

Ellie inwardly cringed. She hadn't summoned Alice. Her reasons for being out and about today had nothing to do with shopping. "She was indisposed."

He arched an eyebrow. "No chaperone? Shocking, even for you, Ellie."

"There is no need to see me home."

"I beg to differ."

He took her arm and led her out of the shop. It was easier to let him have his way than to fight him in public. She'd gotten what she came for. Her meeting with Violet had taken place and information exchanged. She could suffer letting Hugh escort her without arousing his suspicion.

He led her down Piccadilly, then crossed Park Lane. Her steps faltered as he kept on his path. "You are headed the wrong way."

He tugged on her arm. "I know a shorter route through the park."

She struggled to keep up with his long pace. Frustration, and a good amount of anger, hardened her tone. "Must you walk so quickly?"

He immediately slowed his pace. "I forget you are much smaller. It must be your biting wit."

"What do you mean by that?" Was he mocking her? She looked up at him. He appeared pleasant and at ease while she wanted to throttle him.

"It means that at times I feel like I am in a boxing ring with you. Not a physical fight as you would imagine, but sparring an opponent just the same. Your tongue can clip tin."

He *was* mocking her. He made her sound like a harpy, and the barb hurt. She shouldn't care, but she did.

He guided her across the street and into Hyde Park. In the past, the tall trees lining the footpath had offered a pleasant reprieve from the afternoon sun on a warm spring day. But today was not turning out to be one of those pleasant days. The sky had turned gray and the sun was hidden behind clouds.

It was too early for the promenade hour, and only a few couples rode or strolled on the path. Between the hours of four and five, the park would be crowded with couples who sought to be seen more than those who desired to enjoy the outdoors.

She was still finding it hard to believe that Hugh hadn't intended to follow her today. When it came to him, she didn't believe in luck or coincidence.

"Shouldn't you be at the club working on your endeavors?" she asked. "Time is passing."

"I'm not concerned. Everything is coming along nicely. So nicely that I decided not to summon my carriage this afternoon, but take a pleasant stroll."

She looked skyward, gaze roving over the gathering gray clouds overhead. "A pleasant stroll? The sky is darkening. It looks as if it will rain any—"

A fat raindrop landed on the tip of her nose. It was followed by a few more, then the sky opened up.

"Oh!" she cried out.

"Come quick!"

He took her hand and started to jog. She was right beside him. Within seconds, they were drenched. Clouds shifted to cover the sun, and it appeared dark as dusk. He led her beneath a footbridge over a creek for shelter. Rain pounded the bridge above them.

Her alpaca dress lay against her skin like a cold, wet blanket. She began to shiver, and gooseflesh rose on her arms.

Hugh's brow creased in concern. "You're freezing."

She shook her head, her teeth chattering. She didn't want his help, but wanted to return home, order a hot bath, and then change into dry, warm clothes. "I'll be fine."

"Stop being stubborn." He pulled her into his arms and held her close.

She opened her mouth to protest, then shut it. He was blessedly warm and she was shivering. He smelled of shaving soap and his own unique male essence.

He rested his chin atop her head. "You've been avoiding me."

She stiffened and made a weak attempt of pulling away. His arms tightened like bands of steel, holding her close. "You've been guilty of the same," she countered.

His chest rumbled with laugher. "Ah, you've been watching me, haven't you?"

Her hands were pressed against his chest. Unable to move, she felt his heartbeat through the broadcloth. His cheek brushed hers and more warmth rushed through her—a warmth that not only heated her skin, but languorously seeped into her limbs. "I have *not*. I just noticed. You're the one who had initially mentioned an invisible rope binding us, then disappeared."

"You're right. I've been trying to keep my distance."

She pulled back to look into his eyes. He allowed the infraction, but nothing more. She shouldn't ask, shouldn't care, but nonetheless, the question slipped from her lips. "Why?"

His eyes flared a glittering green, something shockingly possessive roaring to life in his gaze. "Because I've enjoyed our kisses far too much. You are a distraction, Ellie."

She shouldn't be flattered, but she was. Heaven help her, she was. All along, she had thought *he* was the distraction.

A crack of lightning flashed across the sky.

She jumped. "Everyone has fled. We should not be alone together." The park looked gray, dreary, and abandoned. The riders had long since ridden away. The strolling couples had fled to their waiting carriages or nearby homes. Even the tall trees seemed faded and washed out as the oncoming mist bled into the park.

They were alone, caught beneath a footbridge in the middle of an afternoon rainstorm.

She glanced up at Hugh to find him staring at her. Her gaze lowered to his mouth. Oh God. She wanted to kiss him again. What was wrong with her?

She was drenched, her gown indecently clinging to her body, and pressed against him. He was just as soaked, only he wasn't cold, but hot. She was achingly aware of every inch of contact.

"Deveril?" she asked, her voice sounding weak to her own ears.

"It's Hugh. Call me Hugh like you used to years ago."

Unbidden memories returned in a rush. His striking features looked even better now. His wet hair clung to him, and his lashes—long and dark—glistened from the rain.

How was it he appeared more attractive, while she must look a mess? She could only imagine what her sodden and tangled curls looked like. It wasn't fair.

"This is wrong in many ways." She tried to recall the incident in Lady Emberly's garden party to firm her resolve but failed. He was with her here and now, and she wanted to seize the moment no matter how wrong. There was too much tempting heat in his touch.

"It doesn't feel wrong to me." The undisguised heat in his gaze made her breath quicken and her nipples harden beneath her gown.

"Hugh?"

"Ellie."

He met her halfway. The kiss was hot and urgent. She felt like steam rose between the two of them. The rain pounding the bridge matched the rhythm of her own heart. Lightning sounded above and flashed in the periphery of her vision. She felt like she had been struck, in a daze of wondrous feelings, her body coming alive beneath his skilled hands and mouth.

He pulled back. "I can stop," he said, his voice hoarse. "Just say the word and I can stop."

Her heart thumped hard in her chest. She knew she should. Whatever was going on between them was wrong. He hadn't changed in five years. Only she had.

She was smarter now. Indifferent.

Or was she?

Her gaze lowered to his lips, and something inside her shifted and gave. She wanted this. Why couldn't she have it?

"Don't stop."

A primitive satisfaction flashed in his gaze. He swooped down to cover her mouth with his. He kissed her thoroughly, roughly, then moved to her ear. "You taste like summer rain and strawberries. I can't get enough."

His words increased her own arousal. Her hands moved to his shoulders to hold him close. She was vaguely aware of him lifting her leg to his waist, his callused hand slipping beneath the hem of her gown. "I've thought of little else since our last kiss. I've tried to stay away from you, dammit, but I cannot."

She'd tried, too. She wanted to tell him so, but then his hand slid up her stocking, up her calf to her thigh.

Oh God.

His fingers teased her garters. He was inches away from the skin of her inner thigh. Liquid warmth pooled between her legs.

"I've dreamed of kissing your naked breasts, the soft skin of your hip." His fingers slid past her garter, touched her thigh. She wanted them higher, closer to where she ached.

His lips traveled to the swell of flesh above her bodice as his fingers slid upward. She gasped and drew in a ragged breath. Her laced corset suddenly felt too tight.

"You have a freckle here." He licked the mark above her bodice. "A pretty treasure mark. Where else may I find them?"

She'd hated her freckles, but he looked at her like she were a treasure, *his* treasure. Her lips parted to speak, but all thought fled when his finger touched her most sensitive woman's flesh between her legs.

Yes. Quivering, she arched against him. Her knees felt weak, but he clutched her to him. Then he slipped a finger inside her and his thumb traced another spot that made her quiver.

She didn't bother to fight back her moan. It escaped her on a sigh of pure bliss and echoed from beneath the bridge. Never had she believed a man could make a woman feel this way. Her eyes slid closed. She built higher and higher until she was on a precipice of some unknown pleasure, then with a last stroke of his finger, she hurtled into pure bliss.

Her eyes cracked open. Hugh was staring at her with startling intensity. She knew there was more to intimacy between a man and woman, and that he hadn't reached fulfillment.

"Have you ever thought about us over the years?"

The question pierced her fog of desire. Had she ever thought of it? A hundred times. A thousand. All her pent-up emotions after he'd left her standing in the gardens, devastated and hurt. And still she'd thought of him. Of them together.

"Have you?" she asked.

"How could I not? You were lovely then, but now…now you are stunning." He reached for a curl that had escaped her bun and wound it around his finger. "Red will always be my favorite color."

He kissed her again. Passion flared inside her and she kissed him back. He picked her up and pressed her against the brick wall of the bridge, then leaned into her. She felt his arousal against her belly, hard and unyielding.

They had crossed a threshold, but she would worry about that later. He kept kissing her, and she allowed it, encouraged it. Her fingers dug into his hair, and she clutched him tighter. She wanted to confess that she had thought of him.

But before she could speak, his body stiffened, and it wasn't his voice that echoed ominously beneath the bridge.

"Well, well. Look what we have 'ere. A blighter and his doxy."

Ellie and Hugh whirled to see two men with dirty faces, patched corduroy jackets, and scuffed boots. One pointed a pistol at Hugh's heart. "Hand over your coin or I'll shoot."

Chapter Thirteen

Ellie stifled a gasp.

Hugh shoved her behind him as he turned to face the two footpads. She could barely make out their faces from behind Hugh's shoulder. One was taller than the other, with greasy hair and a pox-marked face and beady eyes. The other was short, stocky, and bald. He held the pistol.

"Yer purse! Now!"

Sheer black fright swept through her. How could this have happened? One minute, she was melting against Hugh, and now they were set upon by armed criminals?

Their secluded spot had been perfect for their heated kisses but was the worst area to call for help. Was there anyone left in the park? If she screamed, could someone hear her?

"No screaming," the tall man said, guessing her thoughts. "Or his brains will be splattered all over yer pretty dress."

Bile rose up her throat. The thought of watching Hugh die set a fresh wave of panic in her chest. No, she couldn't allow that to happen. She'd lost him once, but to lose him to death was not something she could fathom. She'd never survive it.

Ellie's back scraped the brick wall of the bridge as Hugh shielded her body with his. Her heart pounded fiercely, battling her rib cage.

Hugh slowly reached into his waistcoat. "Easy, now. I have coins in my purse. You can have them." He withdrew his purse and tossed it to them. A clink of coins sounded as the tall man caught it.

"Now be on your way," Hugh said.

"Not yet." The short man with the pistol took a bold step forward. "The lady has pretty red hair. Don't she, Butch?"

The tall man he'd called Butch nodded. "Aye. Haven't ever seen that bright shade before. Pretty thing."

"You don't mind sharing, me lord. Do you?" the short man said.

Hugh's eyes narrowed, and a cold wave settled over him. "Don't touch her."

The short man grunted. "As I 'ave the pistol," he said, waving it before them, "I don't take orders from ye."

"Wait. Get the lady's reticule first," the tall man said.

"Give it to me, Ellie," Hugh said.

She'd forgotten about her reticule. She slipped the strap from her wrist and handed it to Hugh.

"Here. Catch," Hugh said as he tossed it in the air, but it fell short.

The man bent to fetch it just as Hugh raised his boot to kick him in the head. The pistol flew from his hand as he stumbled back and fell to the ground.

Hugh's movements became a blur as his fist struck out and punched the taller man square in the face. Hugh set upon him with a vengeance, punching him until he staggered back and raised his hands to protect his head.

"Run, Ellie!"

She couldn't leave him. Not now. Not when the short man rose to his feet and lunged for the gun.

"Hugh!" Ellie screamed in warning.

She feared Hugh wouldn't reach the weapon in time. He was still battling the other man.

She rushed forward, intending to kick the pistol away before the short thug could reach it, but was too late. He lifted the pistol and fired. The deafening *crack* of the pistol was drowned out by a simultaneous strike of thunder. Her heart seized, then relief spread through her as she saw that Hugh was still grappling with Butch.

Thank God!

She picked up a large stone and hurled it at the man. He stiffened and looked at her in amazement before touching his forehead. Blood coated his fingers.

"Bitch!"

He lunged for her, but Hugh grasped his leg and took him down. The man fell onto Hugh, and they began to struggle. Out of the corner of her eye, she saw Butch jump to his feet and sprint off into the park.

Ellie spotted more stones by the creek. She hurried to grab another but tripped on her wet skirts and went down hard on her hands and knees. Hugh struggled with the stocky man, landing several good punches. She grasped the biggest stone she could find, but before she could smash it on the criminal's head, Hugh struck him beneath the chin with a solid blow. He blinked in amazement, then scrambled to his feet and fled.

Hugh rushed to her side and helped her stand. "Ellie! Are you all right?"

She brushed her mud-slicked skirts. Her hands were bleeding from her fall, and the tender skin stung. She was shaking. "Yes. I'll be fine."

"My God. I told you to run."

"He had a gun. He could have *shot* you."

"No, love. He could have shot *you*." A haunted look crossed his face. Without waiting for her response, he led her away from the bridge and onto the main path. The downpour had diminished to a sprinkling rain. No one was left in the park.

Relief coursed through her that they had both survived unharmed. "We need to tell the magistrate."

"I will handle it. I would have pursued them, but I would never leave you alone. My God, the way they looked at you. It filled me with rage."

Her stomach tightened, and her heart began to gallop once again. "Do you think they will be caught by the authorities?"

"Men like that will commit another crime. I can only hope they are captured before then."

"I'm grateful that you have developed a fondness for boxing," she said.

"I am, too. Although I never thought to use it outside the ring as much as I have been called to lately."

She knew he meant with Baron Willoughby as well as with the footpads.

He tugged on her arm. "Are you certain you were not injured?"

"I'm certain. Only a few scrapes." She held up her hands.

He frowned but didn't release her. He cradled her face, his eyes studying her for injury.

"See. Nothing," she said.

He turned her hands over and examined the cuts. "I wouldn't call this nothing. The next time I tell you to run, you must promise to obey."

"I hope there will never be a next time!"

His expression turned fierce. "You know what I mean, woman. When I saw you throw the stone at that man and he went after you, I felt a panic I have never known."

The look in his eyes was pure concern and something else...something possessive. She tried not to look too deeply into that. They'd both just survived a harrowing incident. All types of emotions coursed through them. That was all.

"Let's get you back to the club."

"Not my home?" That's where they were initially headed. Why change his mind?

He shook his head. "I can't treat you there. And your brother will undoubtedly have questions as soon as he sees you."

She experienced another form of panic. She looked a mess, with bloody hands and a wet and torn dress. She could only imagine how unruly her hair looked. She pushed a damp red lock from her forehead. If anyone saw her—Ian, Grace, or even Olivia—the household would be in upheaval. Ian might change his mind about her contest with Hugh over the club. Even Grace would not be able to argue on Ellie's behalf.

"Yes, let's go to the club."

He turned to lead her away, and that was when she saw the tear in the left shoulder of his greatcoat and the growing bloodstain on the white shirt beneath.

Chapter Fourteen

Hugh pulled Ellie along just as she came to a sudden halt.

"You're bleeding!" she cried out, her gaze focused on his shoulder.

Hugh had been more concerned for Ellie than the stinging in his shoulder. He parted the torn fabric to look at the wound. "It's simply a flesh wound. The bullet grazed me. Nothing more."

"Nothing more! You were shot."

"It needs to be cleaned and bandaged. It's not that painful. I've had worse in the boxing ring. Let's see to you."

Her face paled. "My injuries are of no matter. I must treat your wound."

He gloried briefly from the concern etched on her features and in her voice. Did she truly care for him that much?

They made it through the park to the street at the opposite end. At last, the tall doors of the Raven Club came into view.

He held her back. "Not the front. You could be seen."

He knew that she'd only ever entered through the back doors. Her carriage would drop her in the mews, and she'd wear a hooded cloak and enter through a well-guarded back entrance. She'd always been careful, and he wouldn't jeopardize her reputation now.

She looked at him incredulously. "I hardly care about that now when you are bleeding through your clothes."

Once again, a thrill raced through him for her worry. But he was insistent, and soon they were in the back of the club.

She knocked once, and a slot in the door opened to reveal one of the club's servants. Recognizing her, he opened the door.

"My lady."

They stepped inside. The servant's eyes widened, but she didn't say a word.

Privacy above all else. Rules to live by at the club.

"Please tell Alice I require hot water, clean bandages, and a healing salve. We will be in the women's gambling room," Ellie instructed.

The woman nodded, then scurried off.

Soon they were at the hidden panel. She pressed the latch and ushered Hugh inside.

"Why here?" Hugh asked. Why would she prefer the women's gambling room and not the boxing room or the office? He knew firsthand the boxing room had basic medical supplies such as bandages.

"There's a bed, remember?"

"How could I forget? I thought you and Brooks were sharing more than a working relationship." Just the thought of her with the guard caused an ache in his chest.

Her lips thinned. "Don't be ridiculous."

She led him past the tables and opened the door into the small bedchamber. The four-poster bed had been made, and she pulled back a pale peach coverlet with roses to reveal white sheets. "Sit and let me see how badly you are injured."

"It's just—"

She raised a hand. "A flesh wound, I know. You've said as much, but if you don't mind, I'd like to examine you myself."

Hugh removed his greatcoat and waistcoat. Blood stained the shoulder of his shirt.

"Remove your shirt," she said.

"I never dreamed you would order me to do so."

"Do not flatter yourself. I need to see the wound so I can treat it."

Without further argument, he pulled the shirt over his head. Thankfully, he was right. The bullet had only grazed his flesh, and the wound wasn't deep. Nonetheless, it needed treatment and a salve. She leaned forward, and tendrils of red hair that had escaped from the knot at her nape brushed his arm. Need unfurled inside him—his whole being filled with a fiery longing.

"Those men could have killed you," he said, his voice hoarse.

His fear for her resurfaced with a vengeance. If things had turned out differently beneath the bridge, if the blackguard had harmed one hair on her head, he would never have forgiven himself. Never would have survived the torment of the outcome.

He'd told her to run. As an officer, he was accustomed to having his orders followed, only she hadn't listened, instead stubbornly remaining to help him fight.

"Ellie, will you ever do as you're told?"

She raised her gaze from his shoulder to look at him, her eyes sparking with challenge. "I suppose it depends on who's issuing the orders and whether I agree with them or not."

It was an outrageous statement. He chuckled, but a painful pull of his shoulder cut his laugh short.

Her brow creased. "As far as I can tell, you were the unfortunate one in the incident."

He nodded once, his thoughts returning to their

embrace beneath the bridge before the criminals had ruined everything. He wondered what it would take to get her into his arms once again. "Then I leave myself to your care."

. . .

Ellie tried not to think what could have happened if the bullet had struck inches to the right and had torn into his neck or chest. It could have been much, much worse. He could have died in her arms beneath the bridge. She thanked God for his life.

Ellie bit her lip as her gaze roamed over him. She'd seen him shirtless before, yet her eyes feasted on his flesh. On every hard angle and chiseled muscle. He appeared carved of marble. Her face must be flaming red. She tried to throttle the dizzying current through her and failed miserably. Her knees felt weak, and her pulse pounded an erratic rhythm. She wanted to be crushed against his chest. Wanted to feel more of what she'd felt beneath the bridge before they'd been accosted.

Hugh looked at her as if he had no idea of her illicit thoughts.

"See?" he said. "It is not so bad. A bandage and all will be well."

All was well with him. Her *own* state was a different matter.

A slight knock on the door sounded, and Alice arrived with her supplies.

"I brought everything you've asked for, my lady," Alice said. If she was surprised to find the Marquess of Deveril sitting shirtless on the bed and bleeding, she did not show it.

Ellie cleared her throat. "Thank you, Alice." She returned her attention to Hugh. "We must first clean the wound."

"What about your hands?" he asked.

"You first, then I'll worry about a few scrapes."

She dipped a cloth into the hot water and began cleaning the wound. Her emotions were a whirlwind. She'd disliked him for five long years, had thought nothing but the worst of him, then he'd returned into her life with the force of a summer storm.

He threatened all that she held dear. The Raven Club. Her work with the battered women.

But he'd helped her, too. He'd appeared just when she'd needed him to toss Baron Willoughby out the door on his arse. He'd fought off two vicious footpads, one armed, and had been shot himself rather than let anything untoward happen to her.

He'd protected her.

Twice.

She finished cleaning the wound. Alice handed her clean strips of cloth and the salve, and Ellie proceeded to apply the salve and wrap his shoulder.

"That will be all, Alice."

Alice nodded, then took the bloody rags and left the room.

"You should lie down until we know it has stopped bleeding."

"I'm fine. Your hands, remember?" He took the remaining clean cloths, dipped them in the water, and cleansed the scrapes on her hands.

She glanced at his hair. The chestnut brown was streaked with gold. She longed to run her fingers through the thick locks. Her memories of what had happened in the park before the criminals had come upon them were still vivid in her mind. He'd made her feel incredible. The rush of ecstasy was not something she could ever forget.

"You could have died," he said, his voice suddenly gruff.

"So could you have," she countered. The thought was

like a punch to the gut, hard and unrelenting. He'd returned, and her life would never be the same. Just as the club would never be the same for her. He'd changed her, changed her beliefs and desires.

"You cannot compare. Every time I close my eyes, I picture those lecherous men looking at you. Nothing can happen to you."

"It hasn't."

His expression changed, eased, and the teasing look was back. "We never finished what we started beneath the bridge."

She held her breath. She knew what he meant. She couldn't bring herself to admit she'd been thinking the same thing. "You're injured."

"Not enough to stop me from thinking of the way you unraveled in my hands. Your sweet gasps of pleasure. The silkiness of your skin. The wetness between your legs."

Oh God. She shouldn't allow him to speak that way to her. She was his competitor, a lady, the sister of an earl. Yet, his erotic talk only served to arouse her.

Was she a wanton?

Or was it just for him?

"We are in a private room with a bed," he said.

Yes, they were. No one would intrude upon them here. No one but Alice and one of the club's workers even knew they were here. He'd once accused her of seeking to make the club into a brothel for profit.

Perhaps he was right.

The room was perfect for an illicit liaison.

They could be together one time. Once.

No one would know.

No. This was madness.

Then why else had she brought him here? She could have treated him in the boxing salon.

"Sweet Ellie. I've wanted you for so long." His voice was a murmur, filled with a need that matched her own.

"How long?"

He made a rough noise. "Since the day I first saw you."

Her mind turned, recalling her debut. "When you asked me to dance at my coming out?"

"No. Before then."

Before? She had no memory of meeting Hugh before her debut. "When?"

"At the bookstore. You had pulled a book off the shelf and soon became engrossed in reading it. Your younger sister, Olivia, was occupied speaking with the shopkeeper. I stood at the end of the row watching you. Sunlight glinted from a window above and shone on your red hair. I was mesmerized by the vibrant shade. Then I caught a glimpse of your lovely blue eyes and my breath hitched. I wanted to stride up and introduce myself, to meet you, but I lost my nerve. Then you departed with Olivia and I felt an uncomfortable emptiness. I knew I had to find you. I attended four balls, prowling the dance floors, until I saw you again."

Ellie could not mask her surprise. She'd never imagined he'd seen her before that first night they'd danced. Never imagined he'd watched her in the bookshop. Had searched for her in ballrooms.

Violet Lasher was right. The heart was a tricky organ. Ellie's squeezed in her chest. She feared it sliding down a slippery slope into peril. She was helpless to stop it.

"I don't know what to say."

He pressed a forefinger to her lips. "Don't say anything. It is of no consequence."

No consequence? It mattered to her. Everything he'd said today mattered. She captured his wrist and kissed the finger he'd pressed against her lips.

His eyes glinted. He wanted her. It was clearly written

in his green gaze, in the tense lines around his eyes. Slowly, she took his finger into her mouth and swirled the tip of her tongue around the tip.

His stare intensified with raw longing. "Ellie. You tread dangerously."

"I suppose I do."

She stood above him. He tugged her waist toward him and she stepped between his legs. He wrapped a hand around her nape and slowly drew her in to capture her lips in a searing kiss.

She eagerly kissed him back. His kisses were everything she'd imagined as a girl and much more as a woman. Her palm came up to rest upon his chest. His skin was hot and smooth over hard planes. A sprinkling of hair teased her fingers and she kneaded the hard ridges, careful not to touch his wound.

His groan of raw need startled her. Her body responded with tension, excitement, and heaven help her, longing. Fire raged bright and hot as it had beneath the bridge. Her breasts brushed against his chest and her nipples hardened beneath her bodice. Her body craved his touch, hungry and desperate.

He stood and his hands lowered to her waist. His fingers worked the hooks on the back of her gown until the silk loosened and slipped off her shoulders to gather at her waist. He kissed her all the while, distracting her as she stood in her corset and shift. He cupped her breasts, his thumbs drawing lazy circles around her throbbing nipples through the fabric.

Fire coursed through her veins. More. She wanted more.

She wanted to feel his hands on her naked breasts, her stomach, her thighs…and in between them where she craved his touch the most. She was twenty-three years old and had never experienced a man. No one had made her pulse pound, her fantasies run wild like Hugh. She instinctively knew no one else would come close. Here was her chance to finally experience him.

Could she share passion with Hugh and walk away? Finally be with him and not linger over the past, but move on? Men did it all the time. Why did she have to be any different? She had no desire to marry, to lose her identity to a husband's whims. As long as there was no risk of pregnancy, why couldn't she?

She clutched his shoulders, a mewling sound escaping her lips.

He stiffened and lifted his head to look in her eyes. "If we do not stop, then it will become difficult for me to do so."

She stared back, getting lost in his dark green irises. "Don't stop."

"Are you certain?"

"I am, except I fear the risk of pregnancy."

He hesitated, then nodded. "There is always a risk, but there are ways."

She nodded. "Then I want this." *I desperately want this.*

Still he waited. "You experienced a shock this afternoon. I don't want to take advantage."

"You do not take advantage. Cease talking."

She'd learned from experience that life was fragile and could be taken on a whim. A single shot from a criminal could have torn through Hugh's heart rather than his shoulder. She shivered at the thought.

Did she want to spend the rest of her life wondering *what if*? Her virginity was the only thing she possessed that she could gift as she wished. And she wanted to experience Hugh.

Turning her around, he made quick work of her stays and shift until she stood naked before him. His intense gaze traveled her from head to toe.

"Loosen your hair." His voice was gruff, commanding.

Like a siren, she pulled the pins out of her hair, and the red locks fell about her shoulders. She was aware of where her hair brushed her shoulders then her back. Hugh's gaze watched her, his nostrils flaring.

"God, you've lovely. Like a fiery Venus."

He kissed her again, then gently pinched and rolled her nipples.

She was right about wanting the barrier of clothing gone. Pleasure radiated from her breasts to deep between her legs. She panted and grew wetter.

Her hand traveled down his chest to graze his hardness through his trousers. He hissed in a breath. She attempted to pull back, but he captured her hand and pressed her palm against him. Fascinated, her fingers traced the outline. He was large and rigid.

She worked the buttons of his placket and slipped her fingers inside.

Oh my.

He was like steel encased in velvet. Fascinated, she ran her forefinger up and down the length, then grasped the base. His harsh breath mingled with hers. She touched the tip to find a pearl of moisture there. She swirled it with her forefinger, and his groan vibrated through her.

He tossed her onto the bed. She rose on elbows, her loose hair cascading down her back. Hugh towered above her, like a conquering warrior. She became achingly aware that she was fully naked and he still wore his trousers and boots.

A different doubt crept into her head. Hugh was experienced. Actresses. Widows. How could she compare?

"I've never done this before. I may not please you."

His look was utterly male and fiercely possessive. "I have no doubt that you will please me. I only hope to please *you*."

Her heart slipped another notch.

With efficiency, he took off his boots and trousers. Her gaze lowered and widened. He was even larger without clothing. His erection stood bold and proud. She stared, eyes wide.

Will that even fit?

"Trust me. It'll fit."

Her eyes flew to his. Had she spoken out loud?

He'd asked her to trust him. She'd trusted him once with dire consequences, but this was different, this was on her terms. She wanted this, wanted him.

The mattress dipped as he placed a knee upon it, then he hovered above her, his expression wolf-like.

She should feel fear, but she felt an intense satisfaction that she could make such a masculine man look that way. For her.

He kissed her breasts until she squirmed beneath him. All the while his hands lowered down her stomach to the hidden place that ached for his skillful touch. His fingers found her most intimate spot, then caressed the aching bud. Her head fell back against the pillows.

"I was right. You do have freckles on your lovely breasts."

"Freckles are not lovely."

"They are to me." He lowered his head and licked one. Then another. He kept going, spending time on each one. Her core tightened even more, and she shivered.

"See? Beautiful."

He made her feel beautiful. Everywhere. Suddenly, she was grateful for the freckles.

Only when she was quivering with desire did he cover her body with his. She felt his hardness between her legs. She parted her thighs for him, and he settled between them.

She felt a steady pressure, then a stab of pain took her unawares. She knew there would be discomfort her first time, but she hadn't quite anticipated this pain. Her gaze flew to him.

Hugh's breath was ragged and his eyes were closed. He didn't look like he was enjoying this part, either.

She tried to squirm.

His hands clamped on her hips to hold her still. "Don't."

"I have to move."

"Not yet."

He pressed forward another inch. How was she not to move?

He kissed her forehead, her eyelids, her lips, all the while whispering words of praise. Her muscles eased a bit.

Then he thrust his hips until he was fully embedded inside her.

He captured her gasp with his lips. "Easy, love."

His biceps bunched and the muscles of his neck strained. She felt him shudder. Was he in as much discomfort?

Then he kissed her again and his chest brushed against her breasts. He moved his hips. The pain faded, and just as surprisingly, the pleasure returned. With each small thrust of his hips, her need sparked and grew until she was matching his movements. He increased his tempo, thrusting deeper each time. She soon grew desperate and dug her nails into his back.

She felt it now. The growing need in her body that only Hugh could ease. Her eyes met his, and the fierce desire combined with the possessive longing in his gaze made her heart nearly burst. This was what true intimacy felt like, not just a physical craving, but an emotional one that tugged at her soul. Helpless to separate the two needs, she embraced the connection. They rode the wave as pleasure built deep inside her. Each thrust brought her closer and closer until she unraveled in his arms and mewled her pleasure. With two more thrusts, Hugh followed, and she felt the spurt of hot liquid across her belly.

He held her close. She rested her head on his chest and could feel the strong beat of his heart as she caught her own breath. Then he rose and returned with a cloth to cleanse her of the evidence of their lovemaking. She sat up when he was finished.

"Where do you think you're going?" He joined her on the bed and gathered her in his arms.

She'd thought she could exorcise Hugh from her mind and body. She realized her mistake.

Could she risk her heart and hope for more?

Chapter Fifteen

Hugh ran his hand across Ellie's smooth hip and then along her taut stomach. She was facing him, her soft breath caressing his neck. Strands of red hair streaked across the pillow and on his arm. Like a bright sunset, the color had bewitched him the first time he'd seen it. She shifted and slipped a leg between his. He'd dreamed of this moment, of slowly undressing her and taking her.

She'd surpassed all his expectations, and he was still reeling from their lovemaking. Her genuine concern over his injury had caused an unfamiliar swelling of his heart with tenderness and reverence. And when her hot gaze had traveled over his naked chest, her fascination had sparked an already insidious hunger inside him. He'd once believed Ellie Swift would be passionate in bed. He'd been right, but there had been so much more…

She was giving and generous and had eagerly slipped into his embrace to gift him with her innocence. She'd possessed his thoughts for more time than any other. The girl from his youth. The girl he'd let go to save.

Truth be told, he'd never gotten over her.

His fascination, it seemed, was increasing.

He was put in an impossible situation. Now that he had finally made love to her, his lust hadn't been sated but had only heightened. Worse was his inexplicable need to keep her beside him, to make her blue eyes widen in wonder at his touch, and to experience her brilliant smile and tinkling laugher once again.

For a startling instant, he wondered if he was in love, but then dismissed the thought as fancy. He was too jaded, too cynical to believe in such emotion now. His feelings for her were lust commingled with admiration, and he was generally fond of her intelligence and spirit. It made perfect sense, he reasoned, that he was enthralled by her. What breathing man wouldn't stiffen at the notion of the spirited Ellie Swift in his bed?

He'd taken her virginity. There might not have been words of commitment between them, but Hugh took his honor seriously.

It had been five long years. His father was dead. His miserable mother, the dowager, was rusticating in the country and no longer held influence over him. He had inherited the marquessate and all the lands and fortune that went with it. He'd also become his own man and had wisely invested in the London Stock Exchange and made his own fortune as he was serving his army commission. He was not beholden to anyone.

He was a man different from the one he'd been when he'd first met Ellie. And she had grown into a very different woman. A woman who had become even more bewitching.

He kissed the top of her head and stroked her shoulder. Her skin was so smooth, like fine porcelain.

No one he'd been with could compare with Ellie. He wanted a future with her, but the past stood in the way. Hope lifted his spirits. He could finally confess. After their shared intimacy, things had shifted between them, and she would understand. She would *have* to. Their rivalry over the Raven Club would be moot. She needn't feel like she had to succeed or risk spinsterhood.

He stroked her arm up and down. "Ellie, there's something I want to tell you. Something I've kept to myself for a long while."

She lifted her head, her blue eyes bright.

"That day that you found me with Isabelle, Lady Fabry," he said.

Her expression instantly turned wary. He didn't want to make her uneasy, but the truth would free them both. "That day. I had no interest in her. She had been pursuing me. I only wanted you."

Her body had stiffened against him. He didn't like it.

"Then why did you kiss her?" she asked.

"My father and mother, they were adamantly against our union."

Her eyebrows furrowed. "Why?"

He let out a held-in breath. "The rumors about the earl, your brother." He didn't want to say it, but the truth was long overdue. "About him murdering his brother so that he could inherit the earldom."

She sat up. "They aren't true."

In her surprise, she forgot to clasp the sheet and her breasts were revealed to his hungry gaze.

He forced himself to look away from the tempting vision and meet her eyes. He sat up to face her. "I know that. But my parents, the marquess and the marchioness, they feared scandal. It was also known that Ian owned the Raven Club."

She realized she was exposed and raised the sheet to cover herself. "I thought you were different. That you knew the rumors had no merit but were the result of cruel and vicious gossips."

"I knew then as I do now."

"Then why?"

This was the difficult part to explain. He had just turned eighteen and hadn't known his future. Hadn't yet grown into the man he was today. He'd had no control over his life then, and he'd resented every second of it. "My parents were coldhearted and cared naught but for themselves. They promised to leave me penniless. I did not want to do that to you. You are an earl's sister. You were born and raised in luxury. How could I be selfish and take you away?"

"Ian would have provided for us until then."

Old feelings of remorse and shame arose in a flash. "I did *not* want to beg to your brother. I wanted better for you." It had been bad enough he'd had no say with his father. If he'd been indebted to Ellie's brother, he would have given over the remaining control of his life.

"So you purposely kissed Isabelle and arranged for me to see it?" The accusation hung in the air like a frigid mist.

"She kissed me, and although I did not fight her, I thought it would be easier if you walked away rather than if I broke your heart."

Her eyes blazed, and she looked like she wanted to hit him. "You fool! You did break my heart."

Frustration roiled in his gut. "Don't you understand? I did what was best for you. To protect you."

"That's the problem, isn't it? You do what *you* think is best, not what I consider best. You should have told me. We could have found a way together. Instead, you let me grieve for years. Years!"

This was not going the way he'd planned. Ellie was looking at him with more hatred than when she'd first learned he wanted the Raven Club for himself. Why couldn't she see?

Why couldn't she understand he had done what needed

to be done?

"Ellie. There is no need to grieve now. We can continue as we had years ago." He reached for her, but she scrambled to the opposite side of the bed and clutched the sheet to her.

"You expect me to forget everything and leap into your arms now?" Her eyes were large blue orbs of disbelief.

He hesitated, more unsure than before. "Yes, it is my hope. Don't you see? You can even give up your pursuit of the Raven Club."

Her face fell, and her expression veered from anguish to anger in a flash. "Give up the Raven? Is that what this is all about?"

"No. You misunderstand. This is about us. The past."

Her knuckles turned white where she clutched the sheet to her chest. She left the bed, dragging the sheet with her. "Get out."

He froze. A cold knot began to unfurl in his chest and spread to his limbs. "You are being unreasonable," he said, keeping his voice low.

"No. I'm not. You need to leave. Now."

His stomach felt as if someone had hollowed it out with a dull knife. Somehow, telling her had been a horrible mistake. He'd thought he could make things better between them, that she would realize she could trust him. Instead, he'd achieved the opposite result. She looked at him with utter disdain.

Without a word, he put on his trousers and boots. He turned to her. She looked so small and vulnerable standing by the bed. "I'll always do whatever it takes to protect you."

"Out!"

He slipped the bloody shirt over his head. Not bothering to wear the rest of his clothing, he grabbed his coat and waistcoat and left the room.

Chapter Sixteen

"Grace has been waiting for you," Ian said as he sat by his wife's bedside.

"I came as soon as I could, and I brought Grace a book," Ellie said, a leather-bound book in her arms.

Grace smiled in greeting and motioned Ellie to her side. "Wonderful. Ian just finished reading *Romeo and Juliet*."

Ellie leveled a somber look at her brother. "I thought that a bad choice, Ian."

Ian shrugged. "Grace enjoyed the play and cried at the end."

"That's because it's horribly depressing. Have you no sense, brother?"

Ian ignored the barb and stood and kissed Ellie's cheek. "What have you brought?" He snatched the book from her hands before she had a chance to blink. "Jonathan Swift's *Gulliver's Travels*?"

"It's one of my favorites," Ellie said.

Ian cocked a dark eyebrow. "Where six-inch-tall Lilliputians tie up a full-size man?"

"It sounds charming," Grace said.

"Hmm," Ian said. "First you want to run the Raven Club, now you choose to read this to my wife. Should I be concerned, Ellie?"

Ellie smiled sweetly. "No more than usual."

Ian rolled his eyes. "Brooks has updated us. You are working on a women's gambling room, and the marquess is expanding the boxing salon and plans to increase the number of matches."

Ellie shrugged and hoped she gave off an appearance of indifference. "My efforts will be more lucrative." She could only hope so. Too much was at risk, including Lady Willoughby's future.

"We shall see. Time is passing. You both have only one more week," Ian pointed out.

"I'm not concerned," Ellie said.

Grace shifted against the cushions. "Leave us to our ladies' talk, Ian."

"With pleasure." Ian fluffed Grace's pillows and raised her hand to brush a kiss across her knuckles. "If you require anything, don't forget to ring the bell, my love."

Ellie watched the display of affection. Her heart felt like it was bleeding after her afternoon with Hugh. Could that heated encounter have actually occurred? She still couldn't believe they'd been together. The sweetness of his touch and lovemaking had been tainted by his confession.

As soon as Ian left, Ellie pulled up a chair and offered a weak smile. "Shall I read to you?"

"No. Ian has been reading. I'd prefer conversation," Grace said.

Ellie lowered the book on her lap. Reading would have been easier. She didn't want to talk. She didn't trust her voice not to crack in anguish. She swallowed and cleared her throat. "What does Mrs. Henderson say about the babe?"

"The babe has yet to turn."

In a flash, Ellie's melancholy vanished and was replaced with concern for her sister-in-law. "Oh, Grace."

"But she has hopes the babe will cooperate. Mrs. Henderson assures me there is still time. And if the babe fails to turn, then she has delivered difficult births. Meanwhile, I am to stay in bed. Right now, I'm more interested in the goings-on at the club."

"Please do not worry about the ledgers. I am maintaining them each day. Just as you showed me."

"I don't give a fig about the ledgers. How are you and the marquess managing?"

"What do you mean?" Ellie asked.

"Come now. It must be difficult to spend time in the club and not run into each other," Grace said.

"Oh, that. We mostly avoid each other." Ellie felt herself flush and prayed her cheeks were not turning a telltale pink.

"Hmm. I find that hard to believe."

"Why?"

"I already told you. Because of the way he looked at you," Grace said.

"You're wrong." Ellie swallowed in an attempt to calm her racing heart. She couldn't talk about her shared afternoon with Hugh. Couldn't even think of it.

Trust me, he'd said.

She'd asked him to prevent risk of a babe. He'd kept his promise and had withdrawn before finishing inside her, but he was still untrustworthy. He'd been deceiving her for years.

She felt shattered inside, permanently broken. Just when she had begun to believe in him again, he'd told her about the past.

The true past.

Never had she suspected his parents had feared scandal by wedding their son to her. The awful rumors that Ian had killed Matthew to gain the earldom had haunted her brother. Ian might never have spoken of it, but both Ellie and Olivia knew the damage it had done to their brother.

Grace had learned of it as well. Ian must have told her.

Ellie had often believed that it didn't matter what others whispered behind their backs, only that they knew the truth and loved each other. Family was what mattered. Ian had protected and sheltered his siblings, his wife, for as long as Ellie could remember.

As for rumors of the Raven Club, it was all true. Ellie hadn't given those rumors much thought.

She'd been wrong not to.

The old marquess and his wife had. And it had influenced their son. Hugh had known Ellie was to come to the gardens that fateful night. They had arranged it. Then he'd intentionally let her see his shared kiss with Isabelle. He'd purposely broken her heart.

Why?

Because his cold-blooded aristocratic parents had been against their match, had threatened to toss him out without a shilling? Ellie would not have cared. Ian would have given his consent for the marriage and would have aided them until they could have managed on their own.

But her feelings hadn't mattered to Hugh. He hadn't wanted to go to her brother. Hugh had been too proud to ask for money, and his pride had ruined their future. The only thing that had mattered to Hugh was his twisted belief that he was doing what *he* thought was best for her. He'd never given her a chance and had never asked her opinion.

Even more devastating was the fact that he still believed he'd done the right thing.

Once again, she'd let her guard down, been her most vulnerable, and allowed him to mislead her.

Grace watched her, her eyes sparkling with intelligence.

"At one time, I was as stubborn as you are now."

Hugh had called her stubborn as well. Anger rose to her defense. "I am not stubborn!"

"Hmm."

"Stop saying that."

"I apologize. But please know that I am here should you wish to talk. I am a good listener. Plus, I have nowhere else to be, remember?"

Ellie let out a puff of air. It wasn't fair to blame Grace. She didn't know the entire truth. Ellie had just learned of it herself.

"Thank you, but all is well." Ellie refused to speak of the marquess, not when everything was fresh and she was hurting.

Grace reached for a piece of foolscap on an end table by her bedside. "We received an invitation to Lord and Lady Scotchfield's ball, and it is two evenings from now. I cannot attend, but Olivia wishes to. Will you attend with your sister if Ian escorts both of you?"

"Ian agreed to go without you?"

"I gave him little choice. I insist he do right by his sisters," Grace said.

Ellie's heart was not in a ball, but she could not let Grace down. Or Olivia. "Yes, of course, I'll go with Olivia."

Grace patted her hand like a mother soothing a child "Whatever is bothering you, I trust you to sort out. Only a week remains until we decide who gets the Raven."

• • •

The carriage rolled to a stop before Lady Scotchfield's London mansion. Torches lit the entrance of the magnificent white stone structure. Liveried servants aided well-dressed gentlemen and ladies from their carriages.

"You both look lovely this evening," Ian said.

"I'm anxious to see who is in attendance," Olivia said. She looked exquisite in a pale yellow dress that highlighted her fair hair. An emerald pendant and ear bobs matched her green eyes. Her sister was a romantic at heart and sought a handsome, wealthy, and titled lord who would sweep her off her feet.

The Marquess of Deveril had all three qualities.

He was also the devil.

Perhaps she needed to speak with Olivia about protecting her heart.

A servant opened the carriage door and lowered the step. Ian helped his sisters alight, and they walked up the steps and followed a stream of guests to the ballroom. Ellie smoothed imaginary wrinkles from the skirts of her green silk gown as they waited to be announced.

When it was their turn, Ellie stood at the top of the ballroom stairs and studied the crowd below. The scene was one of melted elegance, as the glittering ballroom and the warm evening resulted in a crush of lavishly dressed people overheated and vigorously fanning themselves in the humid air. A group of people stood by the open French doors hoping to catch a breeze.

A liveried majordomo stepped forward to announce them.

"The Earl of Castleton and his sisters, Lady Ellie and Lady Olivia."

A slight hush fell through the room.

In the past, Ellie might not have noticed, but after Hugh's confession about his parents' dislike of her family, specifically her brother, she was highly conscious of the stares.

Did many believe the ugly rumors that Ian had purposely led Matthew to Devil's Leap and caused his brother's death to gain the earldom?

Ellie glanced at Olivia. If she was uncomfortable with the attention, she did not show it. Her expression was serene and her head held high. Whether it was because she recognized the stares or was ignorant of them, Ellie wasn't certain. Either way, she was proud of her sister.

Ellie raised her chin. They had nothing to be ashamed of on Ian's arm.

Ian escorted them to greet their hosts, Lord and Lady Scotchfield. The elderly couple were acquaintances of the former earl and were friendly and welcoming. Lady Scotchfield had an abundance of curls fading to gray, and her husband had thinning hair and a large paunch.

Ellie accepted a glass of champagne from a passing servant's tray. She needed a drink to take the edge off her nerves tonight. Her mind kept reliving her afternoon with Hugh. Had it really been two days? At times, she felt like it had just occurred and she still could feel the strength of his arms around her; then at other moments, she felt like it had been long, long ago.

Ellie paid little attention to the majordomo as he announced the names of guests as they streamed into the already warm ballroom. "The Marquess of Deveril."

Her head snapped to the top of the stairs.

Oh no.

He looked strikingly handsome in black formal attire. His dark hair gleamed beneath the candlelight of the chandeliers, his profile spoke of raw power and masculine grace, and his green eyes held a sheen of purpose.

"Deveril is here," Olivia whispered from behind her fan, as if Ellie could possibly have missed the announcement.

"So? It is not a surprise." Ellie hadn't told a soul what had transpired in the hidden bedchamber with Hugh, not even her sister. She couldn't bring herself to confess the truth, to admit how foolish she had allowed herself to act with him once again.

Only this time was different from the past. Even worse. She'd given him her innocence.

"Ladies are watching him," Olivia continued.

Ellie shouldn't care, but it was impossible not to notice a group of women speaking behind fluttering fans as they observed the marquess with hawk-like interest. Ellie's stomach turned as she noticed one of the women was Lady Fabry herself.

Not again.

Isabelle licked her lips as she watched Hugh greet a group of gentlemen. Of course, she would be in attendance. Lady Scotchfield was a popular hostess. Jealousy felt like the stab of a knife in her chest. The warm ballroom grew even hotter.

Olivia's eyes lit, and she tapped Ellie on the wrist with her fan to gain her attention. "Gentlemen approach."

Ellie tore her gaze away from Hugh's broad shoulders to see two men. One was Lord Dumfries, the eldest son of an earl, and the other Lord Osbourne, a viscount known for his debauchery.

The men bowed before them, and Ellie and Olivia curtsied. Lord Dumfries turned his attention to Olivia. "You look lovely this evening, Lady Olivia. May I have the pleasure of this dance?"

Olivia beamed, took his arm, and followed him onto the dance floor. Ellie frowned at her sister's retreating figure, then turned to Osbourne. He was tall and thin with sandy hair and brown eyes. Many would consider him handsome. He studied her like she were a filly for purchase at Tattersall's.

Ellie was unmoved.

"You have the look of a scorned lover," he said.

"Pardon?"

"I saw you across the room. I have enough experience to recognize a scorned woman when I see her. I've also sought an introduction, and I knew young Dumfries would be agreeable to dancing with your lovely sister."

Ellie snapped open her fan. "Should I be flattered?"

"You should. If the man with whom you are angry is present, what better way to either incite his jealousy or to forget him than to dance with another?"

She should be insulted, but his honesty was refreshing. Here was a man who would say and do what he meant, even if it was entirely selfish.

Her fan stilled and she gifted him with a smile. "I'd be delighted to dance."

"For which purpose? Jealousy, or to simply forget for the evening?"

Her answer was unhesitant. "To forget."

Chapter Seventeen

She was dancing with Lord Osbourne.

Hugh had spotted Ellie as soon as he stepped foot on the ballroom floor. Her red hair was like a beacon, drawing him in like a drowning man. She looked stunning in a green gown of hugging silk. Her hair had been styled in an elegant chiffon with curls framing her face. A green emerald was nestled between her breasts in her low-cut bodice. He recalled her soft flesh, her strawberry-tipped nipples that had him salivating to lick and lave, her soft cries as she reached her peak.

He'd been starving for a glimpse of her. For two days, she'd isolated herself in the office of the Raven Club and had rarely ventured out.

Hugh had tried to focus on his work, tried to push her from his overheated mind. The additional boxing matches had started, and he'd extended invitations for champions Tom Crib, Bill Richmond, and Gentleman Jackson to attend. Everything was going according to plan. If only he could focus on his goal to win the club.

Christ. She'd gotten under his skin. Again.

And here she was dancing with the most disreputable rake in all of London. Hugh's own reputation paled in comparison to Osbourne's.

"Lord Deveril?"

Hugh reluctantly tore his gaze away from Ellie toward the feminine voice to see Lady Fabry standing before him. She curtsied, showing a good amount of cleavage, then slowly rose to meet his gaze.

"We did not have ample time to converse at Lady Emberly's garden party, my lord. I was happy to hear of your safe return from your service in the army," she said.

They hadn't had time to speak because Hugh had been quick to dismiss her. "Yes, thank you." He looked over her shoulder and tried to keep his eyes on Ellie and Osbourne.

Isabelle cocked her head and studied him like he were an interesting piece in a curiosity cabinet. "You haven't changed in appearance, my lord."

"It has only been five years."

"Much can change in that time, don't you agree?"

"Yes, you are married. Lord Fabry, correct?"

An expression flashed in her eyes then was gone. "Lord Fabry just celebrated his seventieth birthday."

The difference in their ages was as clear as the gleam of interest in her eyes as she looked at him.

"Birthday wishes to your husband," Hugh said.

He glanced at the dance floor. Ellie laughed at something Osbourne said as they met and parted with the quadrille. He couldn't hear the tinkle of laughter, but he could feel it deep in his bones. Damn.

The dance ended, and the orchestra played a different tune.

The waltz.

Of all the rotten luck. Hugh watched helplessly as

Osbourne took Ellie in his arms and whirled her across the dance floor. She smiled up at him, and jealousy reared like a hungry beast inside him.

Hugh's fingers clenched at his sides. He wanted to stride up to the couple, wrench Osbourne away, and punch the man square in the nose.

Just then, the couple spun and Ellie looked up, making eye contact with him. Her gaze darted to Lady Fabry standing close to him, her hand on his arm.

A flicker of emotion passed over Ellie's face—pain, resentment—but she turned away as the dance continued.

No. This is not as it seems.

"I've thought of you over the years."

"What?" Hugh turned to Lady Fabry, his brow drawn.

"I've thought of you," she said, smiling coyly. "Of what occurred in the gardens between us. Our kiss."

Lady Fabry's words fell on deaf ears. All he heard were the strains of the orchestra as they slowed, then ceased. Hugh watched, helpless, as Osbourne escorted Ellie out the open French doors onto the terrace.

A raging jealousy overtook Hugh. *Not on your life, Osbourne.*

Lady Fabry stepped closer and tapped Hugh's chest with her fan. "It's quite stuffy in here. Perhaps you would escort me onto the terrace."

Somehow Hugh retained his affability, but there was distinct hardening of his voice. "I'm sure Lord Fabry would be more than happy to oblige you as his wife."

The lady's eyes narrowed a fraction, but Hugh turned away.

He was going to the terrace, but damned if he would escort Lady Fabry with him.

• • •

"A lovely night for a lovely lady."

The compliment flowed smoothly from Lord Osbourne's lips. Ellie saw him for who he was. A seducer of women. She saw, and she didn't mind. He was perfect to distract her from the couple inside the ballroom.

Memories of Hugh surfaced in her mind. She pushed them aside.

No.

She would not think of him and a certain lady together. Pain inched inside her chest, twisting like a knife. She grasped the iron terrace balustrade and faced the gardens, then squeezed her eyes shut.

"Ah, you are thinking of him," Osbourne said, his voice as smooth as brandy.

"I'm trying not to." Denial didn't even cross her mind.

He pressed a hand to his chest. "You may use me to forget him. Truly, I do not mind."

She laughed. She couldn't help herself. He was a scoundrel of the worst sort. But he didn't try to hide his true nature.

Unlike the devil marquess.

"May I escort you on a tour of the gardens?" Osbourne asked.

She gazed down at the gardens. Lanterns lit paths and created a whimsical, romantic atmosphere. The sweet scent of flowering shrubs filled the air. An intricate maze wound through the grounds and offered the perfect seclusion for a romantic tryst. A Chinese-inspired gondola could be seen in the distance.

She knew Osbourne's intent if she allowed him to take her on the path. He'd try to kiss her.

Would another man's kiss erase Hugh's from her mind? The shrubbery below blurred as the thought took hold, like a cold fist in her chest.

"Well, well. What do we have here?"

As if she had conjured him, she started and turned to see Deveril standing in the entrance of the French doors. The ballroom chandeliers illuminated half his face, the other half shrouded in shadows. From what she could see of him, he looked angry.

And jealous.

He had no right to exhibit either emotion.

"Lord Deveril. I should have known," Lord Osbourne said.

"What's that supposed to mean?" Hugh asked.

Osbourne shook his head. "Nothing of consequence. You may occupy the terrace by yourself. I was just about to escort the lady on a garden tour."

"Like hell you are."

Osbourne cocked an eyebrow. "Pardon?"

Hugh stepped away from the French doors and onto the terrace. "You heard correctly. You will not be taking the lady anywhere. I will do the honors."

Ellie gaped at him, stunned. How dare he? "You have no right."

Hugh met her gaze, and a muscle ticked at his jaw. "I have every right."

Ellie turned away and looked at Osbourne. "Pardon Lord Deveril's rudeness, Lord Osbourne. He must have helped himself to too many glasses of our host's champagne this evening and is acting quite boorish."

Osbourne looked more amused than angry. "You need not apologize on his behalf, my dear. However, I shall take my leave before Lord Deveril feels inclined to challenge me to a fight." He shot a hasty look at the marquess. "His pugilistic talents have been widely remarked upon."

Lord Osbourne bowed, then returned to the ballroom, leaving her alone with Hugh.

Coward. So much for using him as a distraction, she

thought.

"For a scoundrel, he has intelligence," Hugh scoffed.

Ellie's temper flared, and she glared at him with burning, reproachful eyes. "Why are you here?"

"We need to talk."

"You said everything that needed to be said the other afternoon."

He outstretched a hand. "No. I have not."

She shifted to avoid his grasp, her fingers clutching the balustrade. "Go back inside, my lord. Lady Fabry is waiting for you."

"You must know that she approached me. She means nothing to me."

"Just as she meant nothing five years ago?" Ellie bit her lip. She shouldn't give him the satisfaction of letting him known how badly the past still troubled her.

Hugh lowered his hand. "I explained what happened then."

"Yes, you did. You kissed her because you thought it *best* for me." She still could not fathom his behavior, his complete lack of trust in her ability to handle the truth.

"Ellie, please. It wasn't like that."

"It was precisely like that," she snapped. "You arranged for me to see you kiss that woman rather than gather your courage and tell me your parents did not approve of our match."

"I didn't have a shilling to my name. It was for the best."

"Best for whom?"

Rather than hear his answer, she spun away, but he stopped her by grasping her arm. His expression was intense, hot. "You may damn me for the past, but not the present. Never the present. Have you forgotten the afternoon we shared together at the club?"

"It was a moment of weakness. Nothing more." Her voice

sounded weak even to her own ears. Unwanted images of their lovemaking rose fresh in her mind.

His stare drilled into her. "I don't think so."

She tugged on her arm, but his hold was relentless. "One afternoon does not mean anything. Especially to a man such as yourself."

"You're wrong. It meant everything to me." Reaching out with his free hand, he caressed her cheek with the backs of his fingers.

Despite her anger, awareness shivered through her, unwelcome. The longer he stared at her with smoldering possessiveness, the harder it became to resist the tiny tremors in her limbs. He must have sensed her weakness and he stepped closer, releasing her arm to press both hands on either side of her on the iron balustrade, caging her in. She had nowhere to go. Her gaze lowered to his mouth, and she had the insane urge to lick the perfect seam of his lips.

"You were a virgin, Ellie. Despite what you think of me, I am a man of honor. I should do right by you and tell your brother."

Her gaze snapped to his, and she stared at him in horror. "You wouldn't dare." Her breathing was ragged, desperate.

"I would."

There it was again. His insistence that he had her interests in mind. Her own mind was a crazy mixture of anguish and fear. "What do you want?"

"You."

"Me? Or the Raven?"

He hesitated for a heartbeat. "Both. If I have you, then we both get the Raven."

She didn't trust his motives. Not when he'd admitted to ruining their past and not giving her the opportunity to fight for their youthful love. There was also more involved than his highhandedness. More that he didn't know and that she couldn't confess. He would never approve of her association with Violet Lasher, let alone how the two of them planned to aid Lady Willoughby.

She was convinced more than ever before that she had to win the club and not allow Hugh to distract her with false promises or claims of honor. And most damaging of all, he did not mention love.

Because he does not love you. He never has.

Another type of pain seared her heart, the deep-seated pain of an old wound ripped open. She needed to keep the ultimate prize in mind. She had no intention of ever permitting a man to decide her future. Never again.

"Promise you will not whisper a word to my brother," she said, then winced at the clear desperation in her tone. He couldn't suspect there was more.

He removed his hands from the balustrade and met her gaze. After a moment of utter stillness, when she was aware of her pounding heartbeat, he nodded once. "I promise. For now."

Chapter Eighteen

The opening night of the women's gambling room was a success.

Ellie watched as masked ladies of wealthy noble husbands and merchants mingled, drank glasses of French champagne, ate the delectable food on a buffet table, and most importantly, wagered on the tables.

The place glittered. The familiar sounds of the crack of the dice across the tables, the spinning roulette wheel, and the shouts of winners commingled with the sights of colorful gowns and the scent of ladies' perfume. All that was missing was the smell of men's cigar smoke.

Ellie had told her family she would not return home until well past midnight to oversee the opening of the women's room. Grace hadn't been concerned. When they attended balls and parties, Ellie and Olivia did not return until near dawn.

Ellie spotted Lady Willoughby in the back of the room but did not approach. Dressed in a simple gown of pale yellow with a bodice trimmed with silk yellow roses, she stood by the buffet table. A simple yellow half mask concealed her identity. She looked young for her years, young and vulnerable.

Ellie was careful to greet her other guests. She didn't halt by Samantha's side until a full hour later. Lady Willoughby was by the macao table when Ellie approached and lowered her voice. "All is prepared."

Samantha nodded, and together they made their way to an unoccupied corner. She scanned the room to ensure no one was paying them attention.

Lady Willoughby grasped a glass of champagne from a servant's tray and took a sip. "I admit I remain uncertain. I'll never see my family again."

"You mean your parents?"

Samantha's brow furrowed. "They may not sympathize with my plight, but they are still my family."

Ellie imagined herself in the lady's shoes. She would miss her brother as well as Olivia and Grace. She loved her mother, although she did not love the pressure the dowager had initially put on her to marry. Ellie had been relieved when her mother had left to spend time with Ellie's aunt in Bath. "Perhaps you will see them one day."

"It's unlikely, isn't it? If they learned of my deception or where I was living, they would surely tell my husband," Lady Willoughby said.

Ellie felt another surge of anger toward Lady Willoughby's parents. How could they not help their daughter, knowing what kind of monster she had married?

But now was not the time to talk of her family. The lady's life depended on her grit and determination.

Everything had been prepared. A servant had discretely left a small valise by the back door of the club. Ellie knew exactly was what inside—a walking dress, undergarments, and a pair of shoes. Violet had left instructions, and Lady Willoughby had followed them and instructed her maid to pack the necessities. Anything else would have been noticed by the servants in Samantha's household who were loyal to the baron.

"Everything will be provided for you. You are to live as a companion to a wealthy elder lady in Derbyshire."

"I never thought I would look forward to being a companion, but the truth is I am anxious to leave." Samantha took another sip of champagne, then met Ellie's eyes. "But all this thinking has made me wonder."

"About what?"

"About you. I know very little about you."

"There is not much to know," Ellie said.

"I disagree. You intrigue me. Why did you never marry?"

Ellie was taken aback by the question. Beneath Samantha's inquisitive glare behind her mask, Ellie struggled not to squirm. "I never found a gentleman I loved."

"My mother never asked me if I loved Baron Willoughby. I do not believe she cared." Lady Willoughby's fingers turned white where they clutched the delicate stem of the champagne glass.

Suitors had called upon her, and her mother would have been happy if Ellie had married any of them. Thankfully, Ian had protested and allowed Ellie to have a say. Her brother was truly a rarity and wanted her to marry for love.

Curiosity shone through Lady Willoughby's eyes behind her mask. "There must be someone you fancy?"

Yes, there is. And he is outside on the casino floor.

Ellie shifted on her feet. Hugh had also deceived her in the worst way. They could have been together years ago. She could never forgive him for taking the decision away from her.

"Do not let my circumstance deter you. You can still marry for love," Lady Willoughby said.

"Perhaps." If only her heart wasn't tainted by a deceiving

man. "Come. It's time to leave."

Ellie led the way out of the women's gambling room onto the main casino floor. It was busy, and men and women crowded around the tables. They passed the boxing room, and excited shouts sounded through the door. A fight was scheduled for tonight. It was one of the reasons Ellie had felt at ease with her plans for Lady Willoughby. Hugh would be occupied inside the boxing room increasing the profits of the club.

She hurried past and through the club's back door. She hesitated long enough to grab the valise left there for Lady Willoughby. "Everything is going as planned." She continued on toward the mews. It had recently rained, and the scent of horse dung was strong. Ellie wrinkled her nose but continued down the path until she spotted a waiting, dark carriage.

"She's here."

Samantha followed Ellie as she hurried toward the carriage. Ellie threw open the carriage door and tossed the valise on the floor. She stepped inside to find two occupants inside, and icy fear twisted around her heart.

Violet Lasher was settled on the padded bench.

And Hugh sat across from her.

. . .

Hugh barely held his anger in check as he glared at Ellie. He was aware of Violet Lasher and Lady Willoughby inside the carriage.

Ellie's eyes were large in the lantern light. "What are you doing here?"

"Is that all you have to say?" he asked.

Ellie didn't respond, rather she turned to Violet. "How did this happen?"

Violet raised a delicate shoulder. "The marquess waylaid

my carriage. I could not refuse him entrance."

The courtesan appeared unconcerned and nonplussed. As if his invasion of her carriage did not bother her one bit. Hugh would have laughed if he weren't furious.

He'd never personally been introduced to Violet Lasher, but men spoke of her in the gentleman clubs. He'd once heard an earl claim she'd been the most skilled lover in all of England. Whether there was truth to the man's claims or not, Hugh wasn't interested in finding out. He had other interests in Violet Lasher.

Ellie turned back to him. "How did—"

"How did I find you? I suspected you were up to something when I spotted Lady Willoughby enter the club tonight. Instinct told me to circle the club outside, and imagine my surprise when I discovered a small valise by the back door and a fine, unmarked carriage waiting outside the mews."

A breathless rage consumed him. Along with a paralyzing fear for Ellie. He'd considered dragging her back into the club by her red hair and sending word to her brother.

"I also knew you were up to mischief," he said. "The women's gambling room is plausible, but a secret bedchamber is something else entirely. I never believed your explanation that women may need to rest."

"You should not make assumptions, my lord," Ellie said, her voice weak.

His laughter sounded harsh to his own ears. "Assumptions? About the bedchamber or your appearance in this carriage tonight with these women?"

She swallowed hard. "Both."

"You are correct. I need not make assumptions when my observations are damning enough. You enter the carriage of a renowned courtesan"—he glanced at Violet—"all the while dragging the wife of Baron Willoughby and her valise, which if I dump the contents on the floor of the carriage, I would not be surprised to find ladies' clothing and unmentionables. Which leads me to believe you are helping Lady Willoughby leave her husband for a short time."

Ellie bit her lip and twisted her hands in her lap.

Lady Willoughby began to cry. "I knew it wouldn't work. I can never go to Derbyshire as a companion now."

Hugh's eyes narrowed at the lady's admission, and his heart hammered in his ears. "You mean to smuggle her out of London? Permanently? To take up occupation as a companion?" His tone was frigid.

"We have little choice," Violet spoke up. "If not, she will end up dead. Men such as Lord Willoughby do not change their ways."

Silence filled the coach save for Samantha's sobbing.

Hugh reached in his coat and handed Lady Willoughby a handkerchief. "I spoke to the baron about his temper."

"Yes, he improved for a bit, but then he found my mask," Samantha said, then loudly blew her nose.

"What mask?" Hugh asked.

"The one I wore to the Raven Club the first night. The baron found it, and he knew I'd lied about my whereabouts. His temper was the most volatile I've ever seen it. If not for Lady Ellie and Miss Lasher, I don't know what will become of me." She wrung his handkerchief. Another one ruined.

Lady Willoughby's whimpering pierced his haze of anger. If the baron had found the mask, then the woman was in danger. His eyes met Ellie's, and the desperation in her blue gaze tugged at his chest. He'd help them carry out their plans, no matter how insane they had first sounded to him.

His voice softened a bit. "Tell me your plans and I will help you."

Ellie remained still while Violet explained everything. They were to drive outside the city and meet another coach, which would take Samantha to the country. Several changes of drivers and coaches would make it difficult to follow her.

"It's a solid plan except for one flaw," Hugh said.

"What?" Violet asked.

"Lady Willoughby said the baron found her mask and he knew she'd been at the Raven that night."

"Yes," Violet confirmed.

"Then the Raven is the first place he'll search for his wife, and Ellie is the first person he will question. She lied to him."

Ellie stiffened beneath his hard glare, but she refused to look away. She sat straight. "I realized this may come to pass and the baron would seek me out, my lord, but I'll deny all knowledge of his wife's whereabouts. I do not fear him."

"You should."

"I can handle—"

"From what I recall, you could not handle the man the first time," Hugh snapped.

Ellie squirmed on the padded bench.

Good. She needed to see the danger she risked to herself.

He tore his gaze away from her and turned his attention back to the other women. "Let us complete your planned arrangements. Thereafter, I will deal with Ellie myself."

Chapter Nineteen

Violet sighed. "Lady Willoughby will be safe now."

Hugh had kept his word. Ellie watched as the coach carrying Samantha rattled down the road and was swallowed by darkness. "Let's hope she finds happiness," Ellie said.

"Let's hope Lord Willoughby doesn't come looking for you," Hugh said, his tone short, then he stalked away.

Violet touched Ellie's hand. "Be aware. He will not be easily handled."

Ellie dug a toe in the dirt. She was still reeling from the shock of finding Hugh inside Violet's carriage. It had taken every ounce of self-control not to flee, but to bravely sit across from him and meet his angry gaze. "I will deal with him."

Violet's gaze held hers. "I know men well. The marquess is angry *and* determined to possess you. A volatile combination."

She swallowed. She wouldn't give up now, not after all they'd been through tonight, and all she'd been through with the club. "He will lose."

Violet eyed her coolly. "Remember what I said. The

heart is a tricky organ."

"My heart is safe."

Mostly. She feared she was a horrible judge of men. She had made the same mistake with Hugh twice. She would not be fooled again.

Hugh returned. "We need to go back before you are missed."

"My family understands I will be out late tonight; they suppose I am overseeing the opening of the women's gambling room," Ellie said.

"My coach will take you both back to the Raven Club," Violet said.

"We will travel with you until we are back in town. Then Ellie and I shall hail a hackney," Hugh said.

The implication was clear.

"I understand why you do not wish Lady Ellie to be seen in my carriage, my lord, but neither is it proper for her to travel alone with a bachelor."

"I will take precautions. Besides, she should have thought of that before carrying out this conspiracy." A muscle ticked at his eye.

Violet nodded. "As you wish, my lord." The courtesan caught Ellie's eye, and the unmistakable message was clear. *Take care. He is angry and determined to possess you.*

He would fail.

Ellie swallowed any protest of the arrangements. What good would it do now?

They rode in silence in Violet's carriage until the distant toll of a church bell sounded as they entered the city. Ellie said her goodbyes to Violet, then Hugh took her arm, his fingers banding around her, as they walked down the street in search of a hackney.

As they passed a tavern, drunken revelers stumbled outside. One took a look at her and slurred, "Where'd ye find such a pretty piece, guvnor? I'll offer a coin fer her."

"This one's taken." Hugh pushed the man aside, and the drunken man stumbled to the street then promptly vomited.

Good lord. Ellie grasped her skirts to keep them clean as Hugh quickly led her away to a waiting hackney. She settled on the bench, and he took the seat across from her. His jaw was tense.

"You're angry," she whispered.

"You're right. I am."

"You think I should not have offered to help Lady Willoughby."

"Little fool. I'm not angry for your desire to aid the lady, but for your recklessness at putting yourself in danger."

She believed he would criticize her motives more than the risk to her person. "We had everything planned. Nothing untoward would have happened tonight," she argued.

"No? What about when the baron comes looking for his wife?"

"I already told you. I will deny all knowledge of his wife's disappearance."

"He found the mask. He'll know you lied. You took his *wife*."

"We will be more careful in the future."

"There will be no future incidents."

She scowled at him. "You are not *my* husband. You have no say."

"You will cease." It was an order, not a request.

"Why do you care?" she asked.

"Because I am concerned for you. And in this, I know what is best for you." The muscle by his eye had not ceased its infernal ticking. He was still furious.

Her own anger bubbled inside her chest. She glared at him, fuming. "Just as you knew what was best for me years ago?"

"This is not the same," he countered.

"Oh? How is it different?"

The carriage came to a halt in the mews outside the Raven Club. Rather than wait for his answer, Ellie reached for the handle. She wouldn't wait for the driver to hop down and lower the step. She planned to jump out of the conveyance as if it were on fire.

Hugh's hand clamped down upon hers like a vise. "Not so fast. We have unfinished business between us." He tapped on the box and ground out instructions to the driver. "23 Berkeley Square."

Her stomach plummeted. "That is not my home."

"You're right. It's mine."

"You can't be serious! I cannot be seen alone with you in your home!"

"You should have thought of that before your recklessness."

Minutes later, the carriage halted outside a massive pile of stone. With Hugh's presence in the confines of the carriage, she knew she had little choice. But she needn't make it easy for him.

He exited first, then nearly dragged her out. She planned to make a mad rush for the street, but he anticipated her intent and swept her across his shoulder like a pirate with his booty.

She expelled a burst of air from her lungs and slapped his back with her palms. "Oh! Let me down!"

"Gladly. Once we are inside."

"You plan to keep me here until dawn?" Ellie asked.

"Yes," Hugh said.

"For God's sake, why?"

She was standing in his library. His proper butler had raised an eyebrow when Hugh had walked inside the marble vestibule with her slung across his shoulder. Her cheeks had flamed red, but the servant hadn't said a word about her humiliating appearance. The butler's only response had been a drily delivered, "Good evening, my lord."

Thank goodness it had been dark out and no one appeared on the street. If she had been recognized…

No amount of explanation would have saved her then. She rubbed her cold arms and scanned the room.

Dozens of books were shelved in tall, cherry bookshelves. A lush Oriental carpet covered the floor, and chairs were situated before a marble hearth. On any other occasion, the books would have captured her interest. She'd love to run her fingers along the leather spines and sit in one of the oversized leather chairs, sip his fine brandy, and read far into the night.

Instead, she faced a tall, broad-shouldered, angry marquess.

"You said I have no right to prohibit your reckless activities. You're correct," he said.

Realization struck her like lightning. "You think to ruin my reputation so that I will have no choice but to marry you?"

"As your husband, I'll have every right to dictate your behavior."

"You can't be serious."

"Why not?"

"You may be a cad, but I never believed you were a man who would force a woman against her will."

At her words, he let out an exasperated sigh and ran his fingers through his hair.

She watched, helpless, as he pulled the thick strands back from his scalp, then released them.

"You're right," he said. "I'm not that type of man. I would never force you. It's just that you frustrate me beyond measure."

He went to a sideboard and poured himself a whisky, then swallowed. She watched where his lips pressed against the glass. He downed the liquor and poured himself another. She should be surprised by his behavior, but she knew everyone's emotions were running high tonight.

She also knew he was struggling with what he'd discovered. He hadn't known she meant to continue to help Lady Willoughby by smuggling her out of London. He couldn't have known a notorious courtesan was helping them.

For some inexplicable reason, she wanted to ease his torment. He appeared like a caged man—tense and frustrated. She knew how physically powerful he was. She'd seen him in a boxing ring, seen him beat off two footpads. He looked like he could use a session or two in the boxing room right now to release his tension.

It was all because of her.

She approached him. He might be dangerous, but she didn't fear him. She'd never feared he would harm her physically.

Only other dangers to her heart.

Perhaps Violet Lasher was right.

She touched his arm. His muscles tensed beneath his coat. "I'm sorry for your distress."

"Are you? Or are you just sorry that I discovered your clandestine activities?"

Her heart tripped a beat at his harsh tone, but she held her ground. "Both, I suppose."

He touched her face. "What am I to do with you?"

Nothing. Everything.

Where had that tiny voice come from? What was happening to her resolve?

"Will you tell Ian about tonight?" she asked.

"Ellie, I—"

"Please, don't. Will you promise?"

He sighed. "I cannot promise. But I hadn't planned to rush to your brother's home and inform him that you smuggled Lady Willoughby out of London and away from her husband."

She let out a breath. "Thank you."

"I fear it's a mistake. You make me weak."

Hadn't she feared the same thing about herself? Yet, here she was thinking about it again. About the feel of her body pressed against him. Her naked limbs grazing his hardness and heat. The way he made her tremble and moan and squirm beneath his skilled fingers as she reached a peak of pleasure.

His finger traced her cheek, then her full lower lip.

The tip of her tongue met his finger, and his eyes widened in anticipation that surely matched the blood singing through her veins. His groan sent a tingling down her spine.

"I'm going to kiss you now, Ellie. Hard. If you don't want it, then leave this room and my butler will summon my carriage to take you home."

Oh God. Her limbs froze in anticipation.

Leave. Leave now and save yourself, your treacherous heart.

Her feet refused to move.

A second later, she was in his arms. His mouth swooped down to ravage hers. The kiss was hard, hungry, and *devastating.* He exuded a masculinity that jolted her senses, and each time his tongue stroked hers, she became more overwhelmed until she was panting, and her hands rose to dig into his hard biceps.

He moaned. Or was that herself? She didn't care. She wanted him with an urgency that shocked her. His lips left hers to slide across her cheek and nuzzle her ear.

"Just tonight. Tomorrow we must act as if this never occurred," she said.

He looked down at her. "Why?"

"Have you forgotten our competition over the Raven Club?"

"No. I haven't forgotten," he said.

"Then what happens between us tonight must not interfere with our efforts. It changes nothing."

"Is that what you really want?" he asked.

"Yes."

After a heart-stopping pause, he finally nodded in agreement.

She was an independent woman, free from a husband's demands and capable of making her own decisions. She wanted him, could have this, one last time. And he'd agreed.

Then why did she feel an uncomfortable loss?

Chapter Twenty

Hugh gazed down at Ellie as he considered what she'd said.

If Ellie Swift had attempted to test his restraint tonight, she'd succeeded. He'd experienced every emotion—anger, fear for her, possessiveness, and tenderness. For a man who prided himself on his self-control—in and out of the boxing ring—he hadn't liked the vulnerability.

As soon as Ellie had opened the carriage door, a breathless rage had consumed him. Worse, he knew that she wouldn't stop her efforts, no matter how dangerous, no matter how much she risked the wrath of dangerous men, like Baron Willoughby, upon her doorstep. Hugh's temper had never flared as often as it had in Ellie's presence.

His eyes traveled her face, the gentle slope of her cheek, her pert lips. He drew a ragged breath, and her unique perfume invaded his senses.

She desired one more night. Could he do it and not want more?

He bent his head, seeking her lips once again. A fire raged just beneath the surface, and soon his fingers worked the small buttons on the back of her gown. The fabric gaped, and his mouth traveled a path down the slender column of her throat to the swell of her breasts. The taunting freckles were there, urging his lips to touch and lave.

She arched toward him and made a sexy little sound in her throat. It was suddenly urgent that he touch more of her skin. Soon the gown slid down her arms, the flare of her hips, her legs, and she stepped out of the fabric. She turned and offered her back, and he made quick work of her stays until she stood before him in her shift. The simple white cotton was both innocent and heightened his arousal.

His fingers trembled as they reached for her, but she pushed him away and removed the shift herself.

Good God.

Candlelight flickered over her naked flesh, over every curve and hollow and luscious dip. Her red hair gleamed in the light. She was a goddess.

His goddess.

He knew that he was lost, and he no longer cared. "Ellie, you are so beautiful." His voice was hoarse to his own ears.

"So are you," she whispered, then stepped into his embrace.

He swooped her into his arms and carried her before the low-burning fire in the hearth, where he set her on her feet. He tugged off his boots and hastily removed his clothing until he stood before her bold, unhesitant, urgent.

They met in a fiery kiss and sank to the carpet. His hands cupped her breasts, her hips, touched every soft curve that was made for him. She arched beneath him, and her throaty sighs made him even harder. She was slick and wet by the time his shaft brushed against the softness between her thighs.

It was all he could do not to thrust forward and embed himself inside her sweet, tight body. Gritting his teeth, he worked into her slowly, in steady thrusts.

"Is there pain?"

"No. Not this time. Only pleasure."

He continued pressing forward inch by scalding inch until she writhed beneath him.

She responded by raking her nails down his back. The effect was like setting a lit match to a firework. He held back as much as his strained control would allow.

Her head rolled back, her neck extended in an elegant curve. "Hugh, I need—"

"I know what you need," he said gruffly.

He ground his hips forward, until he was fully embedded inside her delicious body. Her breasts molded beneath his chest. Confident he wasn't hurting her, he increased the tempo of his thrusts. She became fevered then, matching his movements. Her nails dug into his buttocks, driving him into a frenzy of need, and he almost came then. He grit his teeth, and held back until she…

Her first contraction triggered his own release. Rapture chased along his spine. He threw back his head, tried to hold it off, but the ferocious need to possess, to mark her as his, raged within him, and he came deeply and fully within her.

Gasping, he rolled onto his side. Slipping from the slick heat and solace of her body went against every fiber in his body. Knowing this might be the last time he was with her was even worse. He rested his head on his arm and looked down at her. Never had he experienced such intense pleasure. Never had he lost all control.

The potential consequences struck him in the gut.

She didn't want a child, didn't want a husband, didn't want *him*.

"Ellie, I—"

"That was lovely."

Lovely? That was incredible.

She had only been with him and was innocent in the

ways of men. Surely, she would throw him off of her and rush to Violet Lasher's home if she understood what had just occurred. What could happen.

She shifted to look at him, her blue eyes bright and inquisitive. "You'll keep your word? You won't tell my family about tonight?"

He knew what she meant. She was more concerned about her earlier activities than what had just occurred in his library. The thought hung like a heavy cloud between them. He was aware of her gaze, waiting for his response.

Something shifted inside him, something that made his chest ache—not just physical, but more. He could have what he wanted, what he'd always wanted. He could protect her, keep her.

He'd agreed to one night. What a fool he'd been. One night would never be enough.

He spoke slowly, each word emphasized in its own way. "You asked me to promise to keep tonight's activities a secret from your brother."

She blinked. "Yes."

"Lady Willoughby's whereabouts will remain between you, me, and Violet Lasher upon one condition."

She lifted her head to rest it in her hand. "A condition? What are you asking in exchange?"

He reached for her hand. "Marry me."

Shocked, she could only stare. "What?"

"I'm asking you to marry me. You can have my name and the club if you marry me."

"Why? Why would you ask me now?"

"We suit. We desire each other. It is more than most couples could wish for."

At her silence, he pressed. "Be my wife."

"I...I cannot. Lust is not love. It is not enough for me." She shook her head. "And you needn't do this."

He felt a helpless stab of pain at her rejection, and a heaviness centered in his chest. She spoke of love. He hadn't believed in that emotion in a long time and wasn't ready to speak of it. He did know what he wanted, though, and he wasn't about to be waylaid. "You're right. I don't need to. I want to." He wanted her with a ferocity that made his jaw clench.

"I don't know. For five years, I have wanted to be an independent woman."

She didn't need to add since he'd broken her heart. She'd wanted to marry him once. Why not now?

"Why this desire to be an independent woman?"

"I want control of my future. Surely, you can understand that need."

He could. It was why he wanted the Raven. "What you truly seek is power. You shall have both power and control. You will have everything. My title. My wealth."

"And the Raven Club?" she asked. "Does your proposal have to do with our competition? I can't help but wonder at the timing of your offer. My brother is to decide shortly. Do you fear losing to me?"

His response was unhesitant. "That has nothing to do with it."

She glanced away, swallowed, then met his gaze. "And what of my other activities?"

He ran a hand down her arm. He knew exactly what other activities she referred to. He did not want her involved at all. It was dangerous. Nothing reinforced his beliefs more than what had occurred tonight.

He wanted to deny her.

But he also wanted to marry her.

For a man who'd been in command in the military, giving up control—even a small amount of it—was torment. It reminded him of when he hadn't had a say with his disciplinarian father years ago. Back then, Hugh had been forced by his father to give up Ellie.

Now, Hugh would have to relinquish control once again, but this time, in order to *keep* her.

"I understand your motives, Ellie. You seek to protect those who are unable to protect themselves. Nothing and no one can change your passion for helping the downtrodden. I realize that now."

She watched him carefully. "Truly?"

"I also understand *you*, your need to do more with your life."

"Then you approve," she asked, her blue eyes large.

"I didn't say that. You must promise to tell me everything."

Her eyes narrowed slightly. "Everything?"

"Yes. Nothing you do will be kept secret. I want to be involved."

"And if I tell you and you disapprove? Will you stop me?"

"I must be honest. I have nothing against the women you seek to aid. I even feel deep anger toward the men who harm them rather than protect them. But if I believe there is risk to you, then I must step in."

"I see. And what of my association with Violet Lasher?" she asked.

"That must cease."

"Why? Because you refuse to have your marchioness associate with a renowned courtesan?"

His arm tightened around her. "No. Because she is putting you in harm's way."

"You're wrong. Violet is invaluable. My endeavors would fail without her connections, knowledge, and cunning."

"You will have your husband instead. Marry me, Ellie."

She rubbed her temple. "I don't know. I need time to think. You must understand that your offer is unexpected and—"

He pressed two fingers against her lips. "Think about my proposal, before you make a decision. I can be patient. Meanwhile, I'll see you home."

He was confident that if he gave her time to think things through, she would come to say yes. Finally, he'd have everything he'd ever wanted.

Chapter Twenty-One

Ellie woke in her own bed the next day.

The previous night's events came flooding back. Hugh had asked her to marry him.

His wife.

Years ago, she would have given her two front teeth to have him propose. But things were different now. He'd caught her as she'd proceeded to smuggle the battered wife of a baron out of the city.

She'd been shocked to discover Hugh in Violet's coach. In that instant, she'd believed all was lost, and she'd feared Hugh would have ordered the driver of the coach to turn around and deliver Lady Willoughby straight to her husband.

But he hadn't.

He'd helped them instead.

Then they'd made love in his library. Shockingly, he hadn't insisted she stop her work. Rather, he'd said she'd have his support. But if she agreed to be his marchioness, then she'd have to cease her dealings with Violet Lasher and tell him everything. Could she trust him?

Another nagging question surfaced in her mind. Why did he propose? And why now? Ian was to make a decision regarding the Raven Club within days. Her suspicious nature made her question the timing of Hugh's offer. Did Hugh fear losing the club, or did he fear losing her?

His words returned to her in a rush.

We desire each other. It is more than most couples could wish for. You can have everything. My title. My wealth.

Not his heart.

Could she marry him, knowing she didn't fully possess his heart?

No, he would seek another. A lover. She barely survived finding him kiss Isabelle years ago. She'd never survive him having an affair or taking a mistress, and that would certainly happen if he felt obliged to marry her to protect her or to gain the club. Could she take that risk?

He'd told her to think over his proposal, but she remained uncertain.

The only thing she knew for certain was that no man would ever be able to compare with Hugh. Her body still thrummed from the experience of being with him. She'd felt protected and cherished, feelings she'd never believed possible with Hugh. She'd thought it was a fantasy—she didn't belong to him, and he certainly didn't belong to her. She'd told him it was the last time they would be together, yet she felt a deep regret that she'd never know him intimately again.

The problem was her feelings were changing for him. The past could not be altered, his stubbornness and belief that he'd acted to protect her when she was young could not be changed. But she knew her own weaknesses, her faults, and that she struggled with forgiveness. It was not in her nature to forget or forgive.

Or to trust.

Maybe it was time to forgive Hugh. Maybe, just maybe,

she did trust him when he agreed not to tell her brother about her activities with Violet Lasher. And even more shocking, she did trust him when he said he wouldn't stop her but would help her.

The challenge over the Raven Club was almost decided. Could she wait to learn the result before telling him her answer to his proposal? Would he change his mind if he lost?

She pulled the coverlet aside and sat on the edge of the bed. She rang for her maid, dressed quickly, and headed for the breakfast room. The delicious smell of fried bacon wafted to her, and her stomach growled. She was famished. When was the last time she'd eaten?

Ian was already seated with a plate of eggs, bacon, and toast before him.

"Good morning," Ian said.

"That smells delicious," Ellie said as she took a plate and helped herself to a heaping portion of eggs and bacon from the sideboard. She joined her brother at the table.

"You slept late," Ian said.

Ellie's fork halted in midair, and her breath squeezed in her chest. "If you must know, I oversaw the opening of the women's gambling room."

Ian looked at her. "Was Brooks there to help you?"

"Of course."

Brooks had been busy on the main casino floor, but she didn't need to clarify. She had hired sufficient workers and staff to help run the place when she'd departed with Lady Willoughby. It hadn't been ideal to smuggle Samantha out of London on the opening night, but Ellie'd had little choice. Once Baron Willoughby had found his wife's mask, time had been of the essence.

The door opened, and a footman entered carrying a pot of coffee. He filled Ellie's cup, then left as quickly as he'd come.

Ian set his fork on the edge of his plate and eyed his sister. "Grace and I will make a decision about the Raven in two days' time. It's not too late to back out, Ellie."

"Why would I want to do that?"

"Because I would think a lady would have other pursuits in mind rather than ledgers and ink-stained fingers."

"You mean marriage?"

"Yes."

Ellie's fingers twisted the napkin on her lap. Just the simple question wounded her in ways her brother could never understand. What would he say if he'd learned of Hugh's proposal?

It didn't matter. Her mind was in tumult, and she needed time to decide her answer.

"I haven't found a man worthwhile," she said. Though a voice in the back of her mind whispered that was a lie...

"You won't find him squirreled away in my office at the club, either, Ellie."

She stayed silent. No sense arguing with her brother. At least one thing was clear. Hugh had not said a word about his proposal or what he'd learned. If he'd visited early this morning or sent a missive telling her brother about her secret activities, Ian would not be lecturing her about marriage. He'd be bellowing at her about something else entirely.

A weight was lifted from her chest. Hugh had kept her secret. Despite her brother's looming presence at the table, his undisguised disapproval of her wanting to win the club, her heart lifted.

Perhaps she truly needed to work on forgiveness. Perhaps they had a second chance for happiness after all.

• • •

The women's gambling room was making money. A good

amount. Word was spreading, and more and more ladies and wealthy women had entered through the guarded paneled doors to place wagers, eat, drink, and enjoy an entertaining evening.

As for Hugh, he'd been busy in the boxing room. Ellie had heard of visits from several champions, and she knew there had been additional boxing matches. When she walked by the room, she could hear excited shouts and jeering. From the cacophony, it sounded like the number of spectators had tripled. Hugh had been careful to keep his own ledgers regarding the profitability of the fights, so she had no idea how much money had been added to the club's coffers.

Despite everything that had occurred between them, she was still curious and wondered if her profits rivaled or exceeded Hugh's. For someone who'd handled the ledgers for some time, it was frustrating not to know.

Things had changed between the two of them as well. The wariness was no longer present, but neither had their awareness of each other ebbed.

Hugh hadn't mentioned their evening together or his proposal, but he didn't attempt to hide his desire. On more than one occasion, he'd brushed against her, and she'd experienced a frisson in her veins. She'd glanced up at him through lowered lashes, and he'd looked innocent enough, but she'd suspected the contact was no accident. He knew how she felt. The night they had spent together in his home was fresh in her mind.

He didn't pressure her for an answer to his proposal. He must have sensed her confusion and had said he'd understood that she needed time.

But she knew he wouldn't give her too long.

Rather than be pleased he was keeping his promise, she'd felt a wave of disappointment. It wasn't fair. She was conflicted, and he appeared calm and composed. She needed to immerse herself in the figures on her desk, the tiny rows of numbers that could numb unwanted feelings or distract from the constant whirl of her thoughts.

It was early afternoon by the time she was finished entering last night's profits to the ledgers. She stood, her low back aching from staring down at the books for so long. She went to the window overlooking the casino floor and spotted Hugh leaving the boxing room.

Her heart stuttered at the sight of him. He was dressed simply in waistcoat and trousers. As she stared into his compelling green gaze—the color even more intense against the starkness of his white shirt—she was reminded of her sleepless nights, tossing and turning in bed, thinking of his touch, his embrace, his heated kiss.

She could not deny the truth any longer.

She was in love with him.

The thought jolted her, and her chest felt as if it would burst. She was not one to lie to herself. Had she ever stopped loving him?

How could she not when he made her laugh, when he risked his life protecting her from criminals and took a bullet in the shoulder, when he did not turn Violet Lasher's carriage around but joined them on their journey to save Lady Willoughby?

There was a strong passion within her when it came to this man, and he had the power to unleash it at his whim. What on earth was she to do? There was more at stake than her desire, her heart, so much more when it came to the Raven Club. Could she trust him?

Yes…yes, she could. He'd shown her he had changed. She had as well.

Her heart danced with joy. She'd marry him. She felt as if a weight was lifted from her chest, that she knew she was making the right decision. Rather than face her brother about their competition for the club, Hugh could ask for her hand, and they could both walk away as winners.

Ellie pushed away from the window and headed for the door. Just as she reached for the handle, a knock sounded.

She opened the door to find one of the club's servants. Swallowing her frustration at the slight delay, she nodded at the man. "Yes."

He handed her a piece of foolscap. "This was just delivered for you, my lady. The messenger said it was urgent."

"Thank you." She accepted the missive, and shut the door. Her heat pounded as she recognized the script and broke the seal.

Meet me immediately in the back of the club.
Violet

Ellie's heart pounded. Violet had never asked to see her outside the club before. Something must have happened. Something bad. Was it Lady Willoughby? Had the baron found her?

The thought made her stomach sink. She needed to see Violet and find out.

She hurried down the stairs, scanning the casino floor for Hugh, but he was nowhere in sight. He must have already departed.

Hugh would want to know. He'd asked her to tell him everything. He didn't like that she associated with Violet and believed the courtesan made her act dangerously. In hindsight, he was right, but it was a risk she had always been willing to take.

But she wouldn't be purposely deceiving him. She had yet to accept his proposal.

Making up her mind, Ellie rushed past the gaming tables, threw open the back door, and stepped into the alley.

Ellie did not see Violet's black carriage. A stray cat knocked over a crate and made her jump. "Violet," she whispered.

No answer.

"Violet!" she said a bit louder this time.

"Over here!" a feminine voice answered.

Chapter Twenty-Two

Hugh hadn't planned on eavesdropping. He'd forgotten his hat and had returned to the club to fetch it when he spotted Ellie scamper down the stairs from her office, hurry through the casino floor, then slip out the back door.

If he weren't hidden behind a stack of crates listening to Ellie speak with Violet Lasher, he would never believe it. From his position, he could see and hear the two women through a gap between the wooden slats of the crates.

"I had no choice but to summon you straightaway," Violet said.

"Is it the baron? Has he found Samantha?" Ellie asked, her voice strained.

"Not yet. But he's hired a private investigator, a man who came from St. Giles. My sources say he's shrewd and cunning and has an uncanny ability to unearth information. Servants talk to him, whereas they won't talk to a constable."

"Are you worried?"

"I won't lie. There is a good chance he may discern that the Raven Club had a part in Lady Willoughby's disappearance, specifically that *you* had a hand in it."

Ellie bit her lower lip.

Violet regarded her. "Is that a problem?"

"I...I just don't know. It's a dangerous proposition. We've never dealt with a hired investigator before. Perhaps we should go about this differently this time. Hire our own bow street runner."

Violet looked horrified. "A bow street runner? They will do nothing and may return Samantha Willoughby back home. She will be far worse off."

Ellie let out a breath. "You're right, of course. This time, when Baron Willoughby returns to the club, I will be prepared."

"And what of other women who come to me in the future?"

"I will continue to do whatever I can for them."

Hugh had heard enough. He couldn't believe it. Ellie would attempt to deal with Baron Willoughby and his hired investigator on her own. She couldn't handle the baron last time, and now, the man would be even more desperate and dangerous. To make matters worse, Ellie still intended to work with Violet Lasher. Hadn't she learned from the past? Didn't she realize that she needed his help?

No, she'd never trust him enough. She hadn't accepted his proposal, and finally, he understood. She'd never intended to accept.

This was what she wanted. Not him.

His thoughts were jagged and painful. He should have known. He'd lost his chance to be with her years ago, and nothing could change her mind.

His jaw clenched tight. He might never have Ellie, but he could still keep her safe.

• • •

Hugh ascended the Earl of Castleton's front steps with resolve. It was the morning of the decision, and yet, he never thought he would have to make this visit. Not for this purpose. He couldn't stop thinking about Ellie's secret back alley visit with Violet Lasher. Both women were serious, and nothing would stop them. There was also a strong likelihood that Baron Willoughby would learn of Ellie's involvement in the disappearance of his wife. He had no doubt that if Ellie continued with her reckless plans, things would end badly.

She could be maimed, crippled…killed.

Her actions had consequences, dammit. She had ignored his proposal, but she couldn't continue on her path. He refused to let her.

He lifted the brass knocker and pounded on the door. Moments later, the earl's butler stood in the doorway.

"The Marquess of Deveril to see Castleton," Hugh said.

"The earl is expecting you later this afternoon, my lord."

Hugh tamped down on his frustration. "Please tell him something important has arisen, and I require to have a private word with him now."

• • •

The morning of the decision, Ellie sat on the outside patio and sipped a glass of lemonade instead of going to the Raven. Less than a week ago, she'd planned to study the ledgers and mentally prepare the most compelling argument for her brother and Grace. She would have left nothing to chance.

How swiftly things had changed.

It was a lovely morning, and swans and ducks swam in the man-made lake. A pleasant spring breeze cooled her cheeks. She would accept Hugh's proposal today. Her brother and Grace needn't announce a winner of the club. It didn't matter who won. Together, they would own the Raven Club.

Her heart leaped with anticipation. Now that she'd made a decision, she wanted to tell Hugh as soon as possible. She'd tell him about her back alley meeting with Violet. She'd accept Hugh's conditions, all of them, along with his offer. She rose and paced the patio in anticipation.

Ellie had never excelled at patience.

Perhaps she would visit her sister-in-law and bring her a glass of lemonade. She opened the French doors and entered the house. Just as she passed her brother's study, she halted at the sound of two male voices.

Ian's and Hugh's.

Her pulse raced at the sound of his voice, and her interest was immediately piqued. It was early, and as far as she was aware, Hugh was not expected for three more hours. Why was he already here, in Ian's study?

"I've been meaning to speak with you, Castleton," Hugh said.

"Lady Castleton and I plan to make our decision later today," Ian said.

"I know. That's why my visit cannot wait," Hugh said.

"What's troubling you?"

"Your sister."

"Ah, you think Ellie will win," Ian said.

"No. It's not about the club. Not exactly. It has to do with the Raven Club, but not our competition."

Ellie froze, her mind muddled. Doubts crept into her head, and she stood immobile as blood began to pound in her temples. Why on earth was Hugh here talking to her brother about their competition? He'd said himself, if they'd married, it wouldn't matter.

"I'm afraid I don't understand," Ian said.

"You must not choose Ellie to win the club," Hugh said.

Ian chuckled. "Then you do fear we will find her the most successful?"

"No. Ellie must not win for her own safety," Hugh said.

"I understand your concerns regarding her reputation. I felt the same, but my wife put my mind at ease. Brooks will manage the casino floor, and Ellie, should she win, shall continue to provide instruction from the seclusion of my office. I understand she will have to visit below from time to time, but those interactions will be limited," Ian said.

"You misunderstand. It's not about her reputation anymore, but her safety. Your sister has been conducting dangerous clandestine activities."

Ellie stifled a gasp as dread pooled in her stomach. How dare he! She began to tremble in shock and anger. Hugh had promised not to whisper a word to her brother. Was he to betray her once again?

Torn by conflicting emotions, she bit her fist to keep quiet.

"What activities?" Ian's voice took on a hard edge that Ellie rarely heard.

"I cannot specifically say. I promised her that I would not. But you must take my word. Your sister is risking her safety."

"You cannot seriously stand before me and tell me that my sibling is putting herself at risk, but not specify how she is doing so," Ian said, his voice strained.

"That's precisely what I am saying."

"I don't know whether to challenge you to a fight in the club's ring or admire you."

"Neither. Just be sure you and Lady Castleton do not choose Ellie as the winner of the competition," Hugh said. "There is more… I asked your sister to marry me."

"Indeed? You did not seek to ask for my permission first?"

"Circumstances were unexpected. But you should know she has failed to give her consent, and I fear she will refuse. That's why I'm here."

"I see."

Ellie sagged against the wall as she felt the nauseating sinking of despair. Not only had she not learned from the past, she'd let down her guard and had fallen in love with the marquess. She'd believed him, had trusted him to not tell Ian about her activities regarding Lady Willoughby. She should have known. Deep down, Hugh Vere had not changed at all from the youth she'd known long ago. Terrible regrets assailed her.

Lies. All lies.

He wanted the Raven Club, and in his backward way of thinking, he wanted to protect her. He would use any means to accomplish his goals. When she hadn't immediately accepted his offer of marriage, he'd gone to her brother.

Just like the past, by controlling her, he thought he could decide what was best for her.

She felt a sickening sorrow along with a sharp pang of anger.

She wouldn't stand for it. She wouldn't act the victim, like she had five years ago. No man would dictate her future—especially not Hugh.

Pushing away from the wall, she threw open the door.

Chapter Twenty-Three

Hugh's lips parted in surprise as the door flew open. Ellie's sudden appearance was completely unexpected, and for a brief second, he'd wondered if the earl knew she'd been close by. But one glance at Castleton confirmed her brother was just as shocked to see his sister in the doorway.

"Ellie," Hugh said simply.

She stomped forward, her fists clenched at her sides. Her eyes were fierce with blue fire. "You bastard!" she hissed. "You wanted the Raven all along, didn't you? Everything you said to me was a lie. *A lie!*"

Hugh stepped toward her, his eyes narrowed. "What are you talking about?"

"Imagine my surprise when I passed Ian's study and heard you speaking with my brother. I heard *everything.*"

He shook his head regretfully. It was as he'd feared. Not only had she been close by, she'd eavesdropped. "I'm sorry you overheard our conversation. But you must know how I feel about it. I only have your—"

"My best interests at heart," she finished. "I know. If I

hear that from you one more time, I swear I will find a pistol and shoot you."

"Ellie!" Ian strode toward her, his expression hard and unforgiving. "I had my suspicions, but now I fear they are true."

"You cannot believe him," Ellie countered.

"I can and I do," Ian said. "I ran into Lord Willoughby at White's yesterday. Let's just say he had a few choice words. I've never liked the man, had always disliked the amount of alcohol he consumed and the way he spoke to his young wife, but he surprised me when he told me Lady Willoughby has gone missing."

Trepidation crossed Ellie's features. "Ian, I can explain if you'd just—"

"I did not think anything of it at the time," he continued, "except to offer my sympathies. But I now realize there is much more to the story. You sent Lady Willoughby to the country, didn't you?"

She paled even more. "I...I—"

At her distress, Hugh wanted to go to her side. He forced himself to be still and allow her brother to speak.

Ian glowered at her. "You lied to me, Ellie."

Her lips parted as she faced her brother. "I had no choice. I never meant to lie to you."

Ian's jaw hardened like granite. "I must think of the future of the Raven Club. The anonymity of the club is its biggest asset. If patrons believe they are at risk or the place is not safe, then the Raven will be no different from the dozens of gambling hells throughout London. You put the club at risk, Ellie. As a result, I have decided to sell the place to Lord Deveril."

Hugh had wanted this, dammit. Yet a sharp pain like the tip of a dagger sliced through him—regret and guilt.

"No!" Ellie cried out. Her cheeks paled as she stared at

her brother. "You can't do this. I'm your family, your sister!"

Ian walked behind his desk. "There is only one way you can stay involved. I understand the marquess has offered to marry you."

She raised her chin in defiance as she turned to glare at Hugh. "I will never marry him now!"

Hugh took a step closer. "What do you mean by now, Ellie? Were you going to say yes?"

Fury sparked in her eyes. "I was, but no longer. I can never marry a man who would betray me so terribly, a man I can't trust."

Hugh felt as if he received a punch to the gut. Was she telling the truth? It was difficult enough that she would not get the Raven Club, but had she intended to accept?

Ian pressed his palms on the surface of his desk and leaned forward. His dark eyes narrowed as he stared at his sibling. "If you refuse his offer, then your future remains in my hands."

Hugh knew where this was headed. He knew and he didn't like it. This wasn't what he wanted. Even though he'd been the one to warn the earl about his sister's activities, he never wanted to punish her, only to protect her.

Ellie sucked in a breath as she met her brother's eyes. "What do you intend?"

"You leave me no choice," Ian said. "The next lady who will be sent packing to the country will be you."

• • •

Ellie left her brother's study in a daze. Anguish seared her heart. She'd lost everything. The club. Her plans to work with Violet to help the beaten, desperate women. Her dream of independence.

And Hugh.

A hand landed on her arm. She knew who it was before he turned her around. Hugh's face was tight as he stared down at her. She should feel hatred, yet she felt only sadness.

"I never meant for this to happen, Ellie."

Anger bubbled in her veins along with awareness of the man. She despised her reaction toward him. She jerked free of his hold. "Liar! What did you think would happen?"

"I had no choice. I saw you leave the club yesterday and overheard you speak with Violet Lasher. Baron Willoughby hired a private investigator. Even knowing how unstable and dangerous the baron is, you plan on handling him yourself. And you agreed to continue to work with Violet Lasher."

He'd heard her conversation? "You fool! I was going to accept your proposal and inform you of our meeting."

His brow creased. "Am I supposed to believe this?"

"It's true, but you didn't trust me, did you? You needed to control the situation—to once again do what you thought was best—without consulting me. You have not learned or changed your ways. And—once again—I will suffer for my lack of judgment!"

He reached for her once again. "Ellie—"

She swiftly stepped back. "No. Don't touch me. Don't ever touch me again. You have what you wanted. The Raven. And you've guaranteed my protection by banishing me to the country. There is nothing left."

Tears welled in her eyes as she whirled and ran. She sprinted through the halls, not caring about the servants who gaped, and made it to her upstairs bedchamber and slammed the door. She managed to sag against the wood before the first hot tear trickled down her cheek.

• • •

She despised him.

How could he have made matters disintegrate so swiftly between them?

A sourness settled in the pit of Hugh's stomach during the entire carriage ride back to the Raven Club. He went directly to the boxing room.

She was going to say yes, to tell him she'd met with Violet and that the baron was still a threat, to trust him.

Bloody hell.

He scanned the large room for someone to fight. No one was around except for two young boys who swept the floor.

Tossing his jacket onto a chair, he savagely worked loose the knot of his cravat and tugged his shirt over his head. Both pieces joined his jacket. He grasped the steel bar above the doorway and began pulling himself up, then down. He counted to fifty, then kept going. Soon, his arms screamed in protest. He ignored the pain.

After overhearing Ellie's conversation with Violet, he'd done what he'd had to do, what he'd believed was right. He'd thought about his decision for countless hours before he found himself in the Earl of Castleton's study. Hugh's motivations for confronting Ian had nothing to do with the club, but rather Ellie's safety.

She needed to end her association with Violet Lasher. Christ, it was dangerous enough to send Baron Willoughby's wife off into the country, but to face the deranged man once again and to continue to work with Violet was downright reckless.

Dammit. The woman did not have a bone of self-preservation in her body.

If Ellie had won the club and Hugh went on his way, who would protect her? Who would know to? Without his help, eventually her luck would run out.

His nerves tensed at the thought of Ellie threatened or worse, injured. The baron would stop at nothing to find his wife. His jaw clenched as his fingers tightened on the bar, and he continued to pull himself up, then lower his weight.

Yes, he'd been convinced his visit to Ian was necessary. It didn't matter if she hated him. With Ellie ensconced in the country, she'd be safe from a madman.

Chapter Twenty-Four

Ellie was in a torment of misery. She sat at her dressing table, cradled her head in her hands, dug her fingers into her hair, and cried. She tried not to look at the trunks in the corner of her room. She'd stay until after the birth of Grace's babe, but meanwhile, her maid had been helping her pack.

Hugh might not have told her brother the specifics, but Ian would learn the truth. She had no doubt that he would soon learn everything—her partnership with Violet Lasher, the secret bedchamber, the extent of their efforts in sending Lady Willoughby away from her abusive husband.

Her life was over. She'd never step foot into the Raven Club, never hear the crack of the dice on the hazard table, the spinning of a roulette wheel, never watch a boxing match. She'd never see the growing success of her efforts. Never maintain a ledger. Never experience the freedom of donning a mask, concealing one's identity, and roaming an exciting underworld of pleasure.

When would she learn? Why must she fall prey to a pair of green eyes and a charming smile? The pain in her heart became a fiery gnawing.

He was a rake of the worst sort.

And she had allowed herself to trust him, to love him, to hope for a future with him once again.

Idiot.

She'd be relegated to the country, grow old strolling the gardens in the earldom's vast estate, and no doubt die of boredom.

To think, she had been so close to achieving her dreams of independence. If the Marquess of Deveril had never set foot in the ring, had never barged into her life and seduced and betrayed her, she would not be in this position.

Tears ran down her cheeks. She hadn't been a weeping female since she was eighteen and Hugh had broken her heart.

Twice now she'd cried. Both times had been because of the same man.

When would she ever learn?

He'd won. He'd come for the Raven and would leave with it. She was left with nothing but a bleak future. And a broken heart.

Despite everything, she had fallen in love with the man.

Fool. He had never truly wanted her.

A low knock sounded on her door. "Go away."

"It's me. Olivia."

Her sister opened the door and took one look at her. "Oh, Ellie. Did the marquess do it again?"

"He asked me to marry him."

"He did?"

"It's not what you think. He only asked because he believes it's the only way to protect me. And when that didn't work, he told Ian I was involved in dangerous activity."

"Were you?"

"Yes. But that's not the point. He thinks he can control

me, that he knows what's right for me. Just like he did years ago when he arranged for me to find him kissing Isabelle." She hiccupped as fat tears rolled down her cheeks. "How can I hate him and love him at the same time? What does that say about me?"

"Oh, Ellie," Olivia said again.

Ellie's response was a muffled sob. Olivia sat on the edge of the bed and hugged her as she wept.

• • •

"The Raven Club is officially yours."

Hugh glanced at the document in his hands. He was in the office of the Raven Club with his solicitor, Mr. Isaac Greenstone, and Lord Castleton. Moments before, he'd signed his name on the deed.

He'd won.

Yet he felt wretched, as if he'd lost something much more valuable.

"I trust you are satisfied with the terms?" Lord Castleton said.

Hugh shifted in his seat before the large desk. He felt suddenly parched and eyed the sideboard in the corner of the room. He nodded, aware of Castleton and Mr. Greenstone watching him. "Yes, I will run it as you had."

"If you need advice about the day-to-day activities, I am not far. Brooks has agreed to remain as your employee. He is an invaluable source of information as well," Ian said.

"Thank you."

Ian stood then went to the window overlooking the casino floor. "I will miss this place."

Hugh pushed back his chair and stood. "You are welcome at any time."

"I know." Castleton turned and extended his right hand.

Hugh shook it.

Not a man to mince words, Castleton headed for the door.

"Wait," Hugh said. "Your sister. What is to become of her?"

The earl's expression was tight as he faced Hugh. "She is going to my country seat. If it were up to me, she would leave immediately. But Lady Castleton wants her to stay until the babe is born, then depart."

"For how long will she be gone?"

"Indefinitely."

Hugh stared at him in shock. "You cannot be serious."

"What is it to you? She rejected your proposal. If it weren't for your concern, I would not have discovered what Ellie was up to. Christ. Dealing with a renowned courtesan. Smuggling a baron's wife out of London. Baron Willoughby will be relentless and will use every means at his disposal to find his wife. I'll need to have men watching him."

"Ellie meant well."

"She knew better." Castleton's lips thinned.

"I believe you are being too harsh," Hugh said. This wasn't what he wanted. Never had he intended to banish her from London, from her sister Olivia, from her friends, from everything she'd ever known.

Castleton's mouth took on an unpleasant twist. "Leave it, Deveril. She is not your wife, man, but my sister. I will do as I wish. Now excuse me. I must return to my wife." He opened the door, then departed.

Hugh stood and walked to the sideboard. He reached for a crystal decanter, noticed it was near empty, then went to the door, wrenched it open, and called out. A young lad immediately approached. "Yes, me lord."

"Whisky."

Hugh found himself back in the ring with Bear. To be fair, he'd challenged the giant to a rematch. Only this time, Hugh had drunk one too many glasses of whisky. He hadn't been sober in a week.

His footwork was slow, and he gasped when Bear's uppercut made contact. Hugh fell to a knee, gasping and sweating. He relished the pain, felt he deserved it and more.

The crowd went wild, cheering and yelling for more.

Hugh felt bile rise in his throat.

Don't puke on your own boots.

He pulled himself to his feet. He jabbed and hit Bear in the stomach, but his movements felt slow and awkward.

His heart wasn't in the fight.

His heart wasn't in anything.

He'd spent a week dissolute and drowning his win of the Raven Club in a bottle. He hadn't shaved and had been short with his employees. He knew his croupiers and servers weren't thrilled with the new owner. He'd heard the whispers of disgruntlement and disgust.

Brooks had watched, hadn't said a word. Damned bastard. The man looked at him as if he knew the truth and he didn't like—or worse, respect—what he saw. He was right.

Ellie would suffer because of him. She'd be sent to the country, never to return to town again, never to experience another season or the excitement of the Raven Club. Her dreams of financial independence shattered.

The blow caught him off guard, and he landed on his back. He struggled to his feet, wanting more, wanting the punishment he deserved, when a loud shout halted Bear.

"Stop!"

The crowd booed but parted and fell silent as the Earl of Castleton, the formidable former owner of the Raven, stepped in the ring himself and hauled Hugh to his feet.

"Have you lost your mind?" Ian growled in his ear.

"Sod off."

"I would, but you've done it yourself. Get yourself together, Deveril. *You* are the owner of this establishment."

At the wave of Castleton's hand, Bear stepped out of the ring and the crowd dispersed.

Ian dragged Hugh to a wooden stool and reached for a metal cup and dipped it in a bucket of water. Hugh reached out for the drink, but Ian didn't hand it to him. He threw it into his face instead.

Hugh sputtered. "What the hell!"

"You need to sober up. You have standards to uphold. Christ, if I knew you'd act like this, I would have given the place to Ellie."

Hugh glowered. "Maybe you should have."

"Don't be daft. Brooks told me you'd been acting like an ass."

Brooks. He should have known. The man's loyalty would always lie with Castleton.

"Stop drinking. If not, you will find yourself robbed blind by your workers or patrons," Ian said.

"I'll be fine." Hugh dragged a hand across his forehead, wiping the water away. "Has Ellie left town?"

Ian glared at him, his dark eyes watching him. "No. Not until after the birth."

Hugh wanted to see her. Desperately. Ever since he'd won, he kept telling himself that the outcome was right. Even if things had not ended up the way he'd liked, the country was safe. The club only held danger for Ellie. The baron still posed a risk, and Hugh had no doubt that she would have continued where she left off with Violet Lasher if she had won. It was a mantra he kept repeating to himself.

"Why are you here? Because of Brooks?" Hugh barked.

"No. To warn you. I've had men watching Baron Willoughby. Word is the baron knows that someone at the

Raven Club is responsible for his wife's disappearance. You need to be on guard."

Hugh sat upright, suddenly alert. "Where's Ellie now?"

"Safe at home."

Hugh sagged in relief. She was in Castleton's home, away from the club and danger. Brooks appeared in the doorway. "Castleton, there is a message for you." He handed the earl a missive.

Ian unfolded the foolscap and his face paled a shade. "My God. It's time."

"Time for what?" Hugh asked.

"The birth. Summon my carriage!"

"Wait! We should tell Ellie," Hugh said. "To make her aware of the baron's knowledge until she leaves town."

Ian's fingers tightened on the missive. "Come along then. You tell her. I'll be with my wife."

Hugh was by Castleton's side as they left the club and traveled to the earl's townhouse. As soon as they stepped into the vestibule, the earl took flight up the stairs to where his countess was in labor.

Hugh caught a glimpse of his reflection in a gilded mirror on the vestibule wall and cringed at what he saw. His normally immaculate attire was disheveled. His cravat was loosely tied. His hair was mussed from repeatedly running his fingers through it. He had the growth of stubble on his face.

In short, he looked like a wastrel.

He should have been satisfied with his win. Instead, he was miserable.

He glanced up the winding staircase in hopes Ellie would make an appearance. Just a glimpse of her would suffice to satisfy the ache in Hugh's chest. She may want nothing to do with him, but Baron Willoughby was a threat, and he had to see her, to warn her. Hugh didn't waste another second.

"Where is Lady Ellie?" he asked the butler.

"She is out shopping with her sister, Lady Olivia."

This was not what Hugh wanted to hear. If Baron Willoughby knew the Raven Club was involved with the disappearance of his wife, then he knew Ellie was involved in the subterfuge as well.

"Where did they go?" His voice was tense.

"I'm not certain, my lord. I would guess they'd frequent the shops on Bond Street."

Hugh was down the porch stairs before the butler could blink. He had a bad feeling in his gut. If Ellie wasn't safely within her brother's home, then she could be in trouble.

Chapter Twenty-Five

"Shopping can uplift a lady's spirits like nothing else," Olivia said.

"I hardly think a new bonnet will help." At the expectant look on her sister's face, Ellie lightened her tone. "But I do believe spending an afternoon with my sister shopping for bonnets is a splendid idea."

Olivia's brow eased, and she smiled. "I didn't have the milliners in mind." She hooked her arm through Ellie's and urged her down Bond Street.

Ellie was not in the mood for shopping, but she did not want to disappoint her sister. She was also aware that her days in town were limited, and she wanted to spend as much time with Olivia as she could.

Her heart sank. She'd no longer see Olivia on a daily basis but would have to wait until her family traveled to the country to see her sister. How awful.

They came to a shop, and Ellie glanced at the sign above the door. "Phillips Jewelers?"

"I'd like to purchase something special," Olivia said.

A departing patron opened the shop door, and the two sisters swept inside. The jeweler was busy helping a gentleman with a selection of snuffboxes. Displays on counters and tables captivated Ellie, and she wasn't sure where to look first. Necklaces, earrings, and bracelets of precious and semiprecious jewels of diamonds, pearls, emeralds, rubies, sapphires, amethysts, and topaz were nestled on black velvet trays. Snuffboxes with lids that could incorporate a tiny portrait of one's spouse were displayed on tables throughout the shop. Ellie wondered if Ian would like another snuffbox with Grace's image. A table was laden with a full dinner service of silver plates. Another held cameo brooches and lockets.

Olivia waved for Ellie to join her in the corner of the shop where a selection of letter openers was displayed. Some were plain with simple silver handles; others were inscribed and their handles encrusted with jewels.

"I thought to get you a letter opener so that you can open all the letters I plan to write you."

Ellie's eyes welled. "That's so thoughtful."

Olivia touched her arm. "Oh, Ellie. I didn't mean for you to cry."

Ellie shook her head. "I'm crying with happiness now."

"I promise to write every day. And I shall visit often. Ian will tire of me asking to see you and will no doubt relent at my persistence."

A tear slipped down Ellie's cheek. "I will look forward to each treasured letter and every visit." Her fingers grazed the displayed letter openers. "You pick one."

Olivia selected one with a jeweled handle made of opal. As they waited for the shopkeeper to finish with his customer, the shop's bell chimed, and a man clad in a coat and beaver hat with the brim pulled down low entered and went to the back. Ellie paid him little heed as the shopkeeper raised his head to smile at the sisters and motion them to the counter to pay. He covered the sharp tip of the letter opener with a piece of cloth. Rather than carry a wrapped package, Ellie slipped her small purchase into her reticule.

"Now it's my turn," Ellie said. "I want to buy you a keepsake as well. It must be a surprise. You stay in the front of the shop while I search for the perfect gift."

Ellie wound her way past tables displaying fancy silver wine goblets, elegant candelabras, and more gleaming silver plates. From the outside, the shop appeared small, and indeed it was narrow, but it had considerable depth. She stopped at a table of amber brooches and necklaces and admired each one to decide which her sister would like.

A strong hand landed on her arm and another around her mouth. Shocked, Ellie tried to struggle, but she was dragged out of the shop's back door and into the alley.

• • •

Hugh took the earl's carriage and directed the driver to Bond Street. He looked up and down the street. Gentlemen and ladies strolled arm-in-arm, others entered and departed from stores, while others stopped to look at displays behind large bay windows. Where on earth could two unmarried women shop? The dressmaker's? The milliner's? The shoemaker's?

"Lord Deveril!"

He spun at the sound of his name to see a golden-haired lady rushing toward him.

"Lady Olivia," he said, closing the distance between them in two strides. "Where's your sister?"

Her cheeks were flushed, her green eyes wide. "I don't know."

"What do you mean?"

She was breathing heavily, her voice strained. "We were

in the jeweler's shop. She told me to wait in the front of the shop while she selected something for me...a surprise. She just...just disappeared. She would never just do that. Never. I'm afraid something has happened."

"Wait in the carriage." Hugh ran down the street, scanning the area for Ellie and pushing past alarmed passersby on his way. His thoughts bordered on chaotic as his legs pumped to reach the shop. Baron Willoughby was raving mad, and he most likely knew Ellie had something to do with his wife's disappearance. How long had she been missing? The thought of the baron hurting her or worse—killing her—caused panic to riot in his chest.

Don't think of how he mercilessly beat his own wife.

Urgency made him quicken his pace, and his heart thumped an irregular beat with each step. With stunning clarity, he realized that he loved Ellie. Had always loved her. His desperation for her to marry him had nothing to do with the club, their fierce attraction for each other, or for his need to protect her, but because he could not envision a future without her. Without her laugh, her wit, her keen intelligence that rivaled his own.

Ever since his parents' damning words regarding Ellie's family, he'd thought to do right by her. And after surviving his parents' cold upbringing, he'd left his childhood home and had learned never to rely on another. Love, he'd believed, was a foolish emotion.

Then Ellie had returned to his life, and his youthful feelings had resurfaced stronger than before. He'd fallen even more in love with her, not only with her beauty, but with her intelligence, her determination, and her unwavering loyalty to those in need. She'd turned his world inside out, and he could never return, never imagine a life without her by his side. He needed her to challenge him, to make him laugh, to make him feel alive, to complete him.

And how had he shown her his love? Because of him, she was being banished to the country and sent away from those she loved. Her dreams of financial independence and helping others were now shattered.

He was responsible. For everything. He'd broken her heart when she'd been a young debutante. He justified his need to protect her by thinking it was the only way, but he'd been wrong. Terribly wrong. By not telling her the truth about his parents' disapproval and by hurting her in a cruel fashion by kissing another, he'd effectively taken away Ellie's right to make her own choice. She should have had a say.

And he'd repeated his mistake when he'd privately spoken with Castleton about her activities with Violet Lasher. Ellie was right. He hadn't trusted her enough to come to him and instead had acted on his own. His stubborn pride, his need for control, had ruined their chance to be together, just as it had years ago.

She had every right to despise him.

His heart sank as he realized what he had done. Could she ever forgive him? More importantly, would he reach her in time to beg her forgiveness and profess his love?

The alternative was unthinkable.

He could lose it all.

His breath caught as he spotted the jeweler's. Pushing past a startled group of dandies, he reached for the door and burst into the shop. The shopkeeper looked up in alarm. "Is something amiss?"

"Is there a back door?"

The man pointed and Hugh took off. Goblets and bowls toppled off tables on his mad dash to the back door.

Praying he was on time, he sprinted into the alley.

Chapter Twenty-Six

Ellie found herself thrust against a rough brick wall in the back alley of the jeweler's shop. She struggled wildly and reached out with her free hand to strike her captor, but her blow missed and knocked his beaver hat to the ground.

Shocked, she stared into Baron Willoughby's cold eyes.

"You!" she cried out.

He leaned close, and his expression twisted into a sneer. "Yes, me." Spittle splattered into her face and she cringed.

"Unhand me!"

His low growl made gooseflesh rise on her arms. "I warned you once. Now I want the truth."

Fear knotted inside her, and she struggled to keep panic from her voice. "I don't know what you are talking about. Release me. Now!"

"Not until you tell me where my wife is."

"Your wife? I don't know."

"Do not lie to me, bitch. Or I'll kill you first, then hunt down your sister and gut her like a fish."

Sheer black fright swept through her. The rough brick of

the building bit into her back. Her thin pelisse was no shield. If any harm befell Olivia, Ellie would never forgive herself.

The baron's meaty hand squeezed her throat and cut off her air supply. She clawed at his hand, but he was too big, too strong. Within seconds, Ellie saw spots. Then, just as suddenly, he released his grip. She gasped and took in great gulps of air. His hand stayed on her throat, an ominous threat that he could tighten his fingers and limit her air supply at any moment.

He scoffed. "You have spirit. My wife didn't last as long."

She hated him with a passion. Hugh was right. Baron Willoughby was mad. And a madman was highly dangerous.

She had to act. Quickly. Time was of the essence. All he cared about was finding his wife and he was at the end of his tether. "I'll tell you where Lady Willoughby is, but you must release me."

"One scream and your sister is as good as dead," he warned.

She didn't doubt him. Her mind whirled as she thought of how to fight him, how to escape. She didn't have a weapon… or did she?

"I wrote your wife's location on a piece of foolscap," she said. "She is staying with an elderly matron. The information you seek is in my reticule."

His square jaw tightened. "Get it."

Her reticule dangled from her wrist. She loosened the silk drawstrings and reached inside to remove the piece of cloth that covered the tip of the recently purchased letter opener. Her thumb tested its sharpness.

Thank you, Olivia.

With a flash of silver, she withdrew it and stabbed him in the side of the neck.

His howl of fury filled the alley, and he released his grip to clutch his injured neck. Not wasting a second, Ellie dashed toward the back door of the jeweler's shop, threw it open, and ran smack into a hard, impregnable body. She screamed.

"Ellie!"

Hugh.

Her relief was short lived when she glanced over her shoulder. "Look out!"

The baron was in pursuit. Hugh thrust her behind him and struck the man in the jaw. Baron Willoughby fell back, tripped on a discarded alley crate, and crashed to the ground. A spurt of blood splattered against the alley wall.

Together, they approached to find that the letter opener had lodged fully into the baron's neck, killing him.

• • •

Hours later, Hugh found himself back in Lord Castleton's study. Hugh had sent for the constable, and Baron Willoughby's body had been taken away.

After a lengthy talk with the constable, Hugh had explained that the baron had gone mad and blamed Lady Ellie—the sister of the Earl of Castleton—for his wife's disappearance because the women had been acquaintances. It was an unfounded accusation. The baron had previously shown up at the Raven Club and had accosted Ellie about the whereabouts of his wayward wife. Even though Lady Ellie had insisted she had nothing to do with his wife's disappearance and had no idea of her whereabouts, Baron Willoughby refused to believe her.

As a result, Baron Willoughby abducted Ellie and forced her into the back alley of the jeweler's shop, where he demanded that she tell him where his wife was hidden. When Ellie continued to insist that she did not know, the baron attacked her. The constable had been alarmed by the red marks on Lady Ellie's throat. Lady Ellie had no choice but to defend herself from the madman, but it was Hugh's punch that had caused the baron to trip and fall and kill himself.

No doubt, the testimony of the Marquess of Deveril had helped satisfy the constable. Hugh claimed they never had knowledge of Lady Willoughby's whereabouts, and as a result, Samantha would remain safely hidden in the country.

Hugh had told Lord Castleton what had transpired. Ian had been astonished at first, but he'd been grateful for how Hugh had handled the messy affair. Thereafter, Ian had been distracted by his wife's increased labor.

Now, Hugh waited, pacing the study.

A slight sound drew his attention to the doorway to find Olivia standing there. She entered the study and halted before him. "Thank you for saving my sister."

He nodded. "And Ellie? Is she well?"

"She is with Grace and the midwife. Ian is in the room as well."

He'd never heard of a husband sitting alongside his wife during labor. But then again, nothing about Ellie or the earl's household followed propriety. Wasn't that why he'd been drawn to her?

"I need to speak with your sister."

"Soon," Olivia said. "You must be patient. Grace asked for Ellie to remain by her bedside until the end. Ellie won't leave her." Olivia departed and left him alone to wait.

Hugh resumed his pacing. He longingly eyed the sideboard and the decanters filled with amber-colored alcohol, then pushed the craving aside. He'd been drinking too much. He needed to stay sober.

He needed to see Ellie. He needed to set things right. He didn't know how much longer he could stay in this room, knowing she was just upstairs, and not profess his feelings.

Then, blessedly, he heard the sound of a baby crying.

Chapter Twenty-Seven

Ellie didn't think she could ever experience such a tumult of emotions. She exhaled slowly, her heartbeat calming for the first time. The day had been frightening. First, Baron Willoughby had forced her out the back door of the jewelers and nearly strangled her in order to find out his wife's whereabouts. She knew, without a doubt, that the deranged man would have killed her once she'd given him the information he sought. Then she'd stabbed him and fled, only to run into Hugh's arms. The image of the letter opener protruding from the baron's neck would haunt her dreams for weeks.

Now she was by Grace's bedside, experiencing joy over the birth of her niece.

Baby Catherine made a choked cry, and Grace rocked her. "Shhh, darling. You must be hungry."

Rather than summon a nursemaid, Grace had stated she wanted to nurse her own babe. It was unusual for a lady, but knowing her sister-in-law, Ellie was not surprised.

The rest of the occupants immediately headed for the

door.

"Please stay, Ian," Grace said.

Her brother nodded, pulled a chair to the bedside, and sat beside his wife. Olivia and Ellie quietly departed to leave the new parents alone.

Once in the hall, Olivia halted Ellie. "Lord Deveril is in the study. He is asking for you. You should know, he looks even worse than Ian."

Ellie swallowed. Despite her despair over her broken heart and her soon-to-be banishment, she owed Hugh her life. She found him staring out the window of the study, his arms folded at his back. "My lord?"

He turned. Olivia was right. She couldn't help but notice the difference in Hugh's appearance. His attire was disheveled. His hair was mussed, his cravat loosely tied and wrinkled, and a stain marred his shirtfront. His handsome face looked ragged, as if he had been out drinking until the early morning.

Perhaps he had.

She hadn't taken note of his appearance when he'd run into the alley. Or afterward, when they'd spoken with the constable as Baron Willoughby's body was carted away.

She shivered. Her nerves had been strained then, her mind reeling.

Now that things had resolved, she knew she should limit her time with Hugh. Her circumstances had not changed. She would be banished from town soon.

Still, it was difficult to keep her gaze from wandering to him. After today, she'd likely never see him again. He had no reason to visit Castleton's country estate, not when he had the Raven Club to manage and all of the pleasures of town at his feet as a wealthy marquess. She should be relieved not to see him again.

Then why did her heart squeeze in anguish? The swell of

pain was beyond tears.

"Olivia explained why you were at Bond Street. I never thanked you for coming to my aid," she said.

"You needn't thank me. My heart stopped when your sister told me you were missing."

She halted in front of the large rosewood desk. Fearful her legs would give out, she leaned against it. "If that is all, I must finish packing for the country. Now that the babe is born, I won't have much time."

To his credit, he winced at her statement. "You needn't bother."

"I do believe I have no choice."

A look of distress flashed across his handsome face. "You were right all along, Ellie. I've been a fool. I'm here to ask for your forgiveness."

Her fingers tightened on the edge of the desk. "My forgiveness?"

"I was wrong all those years ago for luring you into the gardens and then kissing Isabelle. I should have told you about my parents' disapproval. Most importantly, I should have ignored their cruel demands and married you. I have no doubt now that we would have sorted everything out together. Even if we lived impoverished, and I know Castleton wouldn't have allowed that, it was wrong of me not to confess the truth. Because of my stubborn pride, you never had a say."

She stood before him, amazed and shaken by his words. If only they *could* have changed the past. If only he hadn't talked to her brother and betrayed her. If only she didn't have to return to her bedchamber and pack her portmanteau. "My lord, I—"

"Please, let me finish. You deserve to hear this. I should never have spoken to Castleton about your activities at the club. Both times I believed I was protecting you, but I should have trusted you. I know it is too much to ask for forgiveness now, but I must try."

Her gaze traveled over his face. His expression was one of wretchedness commingled with hope, and she realized his disheveled appearance reflected his misery over the course of the past several days. She ached with an inner pain. It was too late. Nothing could change her future. Her brother had made a decision, and she was powerless to fight him. She dropped her lashes to hide her own misery. "Thank you for telling me. Please pardon me, but I must prepare for my journey."

He touched her arm before she could fully turn away. "Wait. There is more. I love you, Ellie. I always have."

Her heart pounded at his confession. His expression was earnest and his green eyes full of intent and purpose. Why, after all this time, did he tell her now? She'd loved him for a lifetime, and now it was too late.

"If you do not wish to marry me, then I cannot allow you to leave London," he said, his voice full of purpose.

"My brother has decided," she said.

"You need not leave. I shall."

She stared up at him, her emotions a tangled web. "What of the Raven Club?"

"I no longer want it. It's yours."

Her eyes widened in astonishment. She opened her mouth, then closed it, unsure what to say.

"I will not stand in your way. I will leave London forever if that is what you wish." Reaching into his coat pocket, he pulled out a parchment. He unrolled it to reveal an official-looking document with a seal. "It's already done. My solicitor has transferred the deed to the club to you. Everything is now in your name." He handed it to her.

She stared at the document in her open palm, then her gaze flew to his. She read despair in his green eyes. A despair that matched her own.

She was afraid to breathe. The words came out on a sob.

"Oh, Hugh. Are you certain?"

"More certain than anything in my life. I love you. I wish for you to have everything you desire, even if I cannot be with you. You can have the club and continue to help others. I want you to be happy, Ellie."

She looked at him in awe. He admitted his flaw and had proclaimed his love. Could she do the same?

Forgiveness was a virtue she'd struggled with. It was her own flaw, she knew. But she refused to allow her pride and stubbornness to ruin her future.

She raised her chin, and her lips curved in a smile. "I've been guilty of my own sins of pride. I forgive you."

He let out a held-in breath. "Thank you."

He might have gifted her the deed, but she still had her brother's demands to contend with. Would Ian permit her to stay in London? Would he allow her to run the Raven Club without interference even knowing what she'd done...what she still planned to do?

No. He'd never allow it.

The deed burned in her hand along with the thudding of her heart. Her troubles were far from over, even with Hugh's gift.

"I do believe forgiveness calls for a kiss," she said, her voice breathless.

Once more to say goodbye.

She recognized the moment hope lit his gaze, and her chest squeezed.

She rose on her tiptoes as he lowered his head to capture her mouth. Seconds later, his strong arms pulled her to him. It was a sweet kiss, the kind that melted her bones and tugged at her heart. A kiss that made her feel treasured and, heaven help her, *loved*.

A small thought pierced her haze of joy. Not all was lost; an opportunity remained. But was she bold enough to seize it?

Yes, she was. If it meant finally obtaining the happiness that had escaped her years ago. A happiness they both deserved.

She pressed a hand against his chest and felt his own heart beat in response. Lifting her head, she looked up at him and took a deep breath. "You should know that I've never stopped loving you."

"Truly?" he asked.

"Oh, yes. From years ago. And from the first moment I spotted you in the boxing ring with Bear. It took me a while to realize it, but now I know."

He looked at her in delight. "I wish I had known. It would have changed everything."

In spite of her nervousness, she laughed out loud. "While we are confessing, you should know there is something else I desire."

Unmistakable mischief lit his eyes. "Such as?"

"Marry me."

His hands covered hers where it pressed against his chest, and his eyes welled with tears. "I thought you would never ask. It would be my honor."

"And the club?" she asked as she held up the deed she still clutched in her free hand. "Will you want this back?"

"No. It's yours."

Her heart danced with joy. "It's *ours*. Together it will flourish."

"I do believe I must speak with Castleton and seek his permission," Hugh said.

"Luck is with you. My brother is in a good mood today."

Chapter Twenty-Eight

"It took both of you long enough," Grace said as she sat on a velvet settee in the parlor.

Catherine had nursed and was sleeping peacefully in her father's arms. Ian had a bemused look on his face every time he looked down at the infant.

"What do you mean?" Ellie asked. Hugh stood by her side. He looked just as confused.

Two days had passed since Hugh had accepted Ellie's marriage proposal. During that time Hugh had desperately sought an audience with Castleton but had to wait. Now that Baron Willoughby was no longer a threat, Ian had spent every waking moment with his new family.

"Your betrothal was our plan all along," Grace said. She looked healthy and certainly happy not to be confined to bed any longer.

"Our?" Ian asked, cocking a dark eyebrow.

"Fine. *I* knew all along," Grace countered.

"How?" Ellie asked.

"There was no other reason for you to reject suitor after

suitor over the years," Grace said.

"I wanted independence," Ellie protested.

"No. It would have been a lonely life. You are a vibrant young lady. You deserve a partner. A man who will cherish you and always seek your happiness in life," Grace said as she glanced at her husband.

Ellie glared at her brother. "Were you part of this plan, Ian?"

Ian halted his pacing but kept rocking the babe. She still couldn't get used to seeing her brother handle the tiny infant with such care and adoration. "I have learned long ago to trust my wife's judgment."

"Does this mean you agree to give me your sister's hand in marriage?" Hugh asked.

"Yes," Grace and Ian said in unison.

"And the club?" Grace asked.

"Is Ellie's. I had the solicitor draw up the papers myself," Hugh responded.

"Well, that is an interesting development. But I assume you will both be proprietors. From what I've seen of the ledgers, both of your ideas are creative and lucrative," Grace said. "I do believe it would have been a tie."

"Yes. Both of us tied. Together." A look of male satisfaction crossed Hugh's face as he looked at Ellie.

Ellie and Hugh left the new parents and quietly closed the parlor door. Hugh took her arm and led her outside into the gardens and the sunshine. As soon as they were alone, he swept her into his arms.

"I will impatiently wait until the reading of the bans and our wedding day to make love to you again."

She eyed him with a knowing smile. "Why wait? I do believe I can convince you to seduce me beforehand."

"I'll take that bet. But you should know, we will both be winners."

He kissed her, deeply and with love. Ellie clutched his coat and reveled in his kiss, loved the way he held her as if she was cherished and meant more to him than life. He'd held her heart for so long, and now she knew she'd held his, too.

It was a new day. A new future. For the Raven Club and their family.

Epilogue

The roulette wheel stopped on red twenty-two.

"I won!" Olivia shouted, her face flushed with excitement.

Ian groaned. "How on earth did you win?"

"This may not bode well," Hugh said.

"Oh, let her have a bit of fun," Ellie said.

The family was gathered around the roulette wheel at the Raven Club. It was a special night. They had closed the club to the patrons to celebrate with family and friends.

Hugh and Ellie had married a week before at St. George's church and had a respectable wedding breakfast at her brother's home. They hadn't gone on a honeymoon. Rather, they had wanted to resume working at the Raven Club.

Brooks remained in their employ.

There were hushed rumors that the club had changed ownership, but no one was certain. Many believed the Marquess of Deveril was a new partner. He was frequently seen in the boxing room. No one had directly asked the Earl of Castleton. They valued their membership too much.

Ellie rarely stepped foot on the main casino floor during

business hours. She worked on the ledgers and handled all the behind-the-scenes aspects of the business. But she did attend the women's gambling room each night. As word of mouth spread, so did their business. Ladies and wealthy wives of merchants strived for membership.

The boxing room was doing a brisk business as well. Boxing champions attended regularly, and wagers were at an all-time high.

"Grace is planning a house party at the country estate. Olivia said she wants to accompany her to help care for Catherine."

"You think Olivia will be happy?"

"It will only be for three weeks. And yes, she will be happy. She adores Catherine. And the estate's stables are full of thoroughbreds."

As if sensing she was the topic of conversation, the baby turned and looked directly at Ellie.

"She smiled at me!" Ellie cried out.

"Yes, she is a happy baby," Grace said as she cradled her daughter.

"Most likely she has flatulence," Castleton said.

"Ian!" Grace admonished.

Castleton shrugged a shoulder. "We have not slept well. Grace checks on Catherine in the nursery each night even though the nursemaid is competent."

"You visit the nursery as well," Grace countered.

Castleton actually flushed. "I like to hold her."

"You spoil her," Grace said.

"So? A man is permitted to spoil his daughter. Isn't that right, Deveril?" Castleton asked.

Ellie elbowed Hugh, and he immediately agreed. "Yes. I would do the same."

Ellie gave him a quizzical look, then whispered in his ear, "Would you?"

"I have no doubt," Hugh said.

"Good. Because in little less than eight months' time, you may have to," Ellie said.

Hugh's eyes widened, and he looked at her. "Eight months' time?" The thought pierced his haze of shock, and a thrill of joy filled his heart.

Ellie nodded, barely containing a smile.

"You mean you knew before we married? When you were going to depart to live in the country?" Hugh asked in disbelief.

"I didn't know. I was miserable," Ellie said.

"Thank God you came to your senses and married me."

She elbowed him more forcefully this time.

"Oomph. I suppose I deserved that," Hugh said.

"Are you happy to hear the news?" she asked.

"Yes. Absolutely, yes."

When he thought about what he'd almost lost, his chest squeezed tight. He took her in his arms and kissed her. It didn't matter that their whole family was present. Nothing mattered but Ellie. The future was bright indeed.

Acknowledgments

Writers create stories in solitude, but publishing a book is a team effort. I'm thankful for all the wonderful people who have helped me along the way. I will always be indebted to my parents, Anahid and Gabriel, and miss them every day. They taught me to work hard and never stop believing in myself.

Thanks to my girls—Laura and Gabrielle—for believing in mom. I'm eternally grateful to John for his never-ending support, encouragement, and love.

Thank you to my agent, Stephany Evans, for your guidance and for always believing in me.

And a special thank you to my editor, Alycia Tornetta, and Entangled Publishing for all their work on my behalf.

Last, thanks to my readers. Without you, there would be no books!

About the Author

Best-selling author Tina Gabrielle is an attorney and former mechanical engineer whose love of reading for pleasure helped her get through years of academia. She often picked up a romance and let her fantasies of knights in shining armor and lords and ladies carry her away. She is the author of adventurous Regency historical romances for Entangled Publishing and Kensington Books.

Publisher's Weekly calls her Regency Barrister's series, "Well-matched lovers...witty comradely repartee." Tina's books have been Barnes & Noble top picks, and her first book, *Lady of Scandal*, was nominated as best first historical by *Romantic Times Book Reviews*. Tina lives in New Jersey and is married to her own hero and is blessed with two daughters. She loves to hear from readers. Visit her website to learn about upcoming releases, join her newsletter, and enter free monthly contests at www.tinagabrielle.com. Sign up for Tina's newsletter to keep up-to-date on all of her upcoming releases.

You can also find Tina at:
Twitter: @TinaGabrielle
Facebook: www.facebook.com/TinaGabrielle
Instagram: www.instagram.com/TinaGabrielleAuthor

Get Scandalous with these historical reads...

To Resist a Scandalous Rogue
a *Once Upon a Scandal* novel by Liana De la Rosa

Finlay Swinton, Viscount Firthwell, is determined to free himself of his family's scandal and run for Parliament. But he can't stay away from Charlotte, despite her working class status and Jewish faith that might destroy his chance for success. Widowed Charlotte Taylor relaxes into anonymity until Finlay, the man she shared one romantic night with, reappears and ignites her passion. When those from her past threaten her, she'll have to reveal his secret or go to prison.

Wicked With the Scoundrel
a *Wicked Secrets* novel by Elizabeth Bright

Colin Smith, bastard son of a viscount, has no use for the stifling rules of the ton, but he's happy to play the game in order to sell some of his treasures. Lady Claire's life is filled with dances and evening gowns, but she secretly yearns for something very different. She's determined to convince Colin to take her with him to travel the world. There's just one problem, he doesn't seem to like her much.

THE EARL AND THE RELUCTANT LADY
a *Lords of Vice* novel by Robyn DeHart

From the very moment Agnes Watkins walked into his life, Fletcher Banks, Earl of Wakefield, has wanted her. Agnes is not just beautiful, she's clever and determined. Despite her uncommon beauty, she refuses to conform to society's standards. She's also the sister of the man who holds Fletcher's career as a spy in his hands. And that makes her completely off-limits. But the more time they spend together, the harder it is to deny that this infatuation may be more than lust…

THE ROGUE'S CONQUEST
a *Townsends* novel by Lily Maxton

Former prizefighter James MacGregor wants to be a gentleman, like the men he trains in his boxing saloon. A chance encounter with Eleanor Townsend gives him the leverage he needs. She'll gain him entry to high society and help him with his atrocious manners, and in return, he won't reveal her secret. It's the perfect arrangement. At least until the sparks between them become more than just their personalities clashing.

Made in the USA
Coppell, TX
16 June 2022

78911310R00146